THE EAGLE

OF DECEIT

MILKANA N. MINGELS

For AJ

Once upon a time, a young boy asked his grandfather, "Grandfather, is it true that one of your friends once made a pact with the Devil?"

"Well, yes, he did," said Goran, "you see, everything was different back then, even the Devil. But this is not the worst my friend could have done. He could have made a pact with a samodiva."

"A samodiva?" exclaimed the boy.

"Oh, yes!" said Goran, "but this is a story for another time."

CONTENTS

1   Vodnik   1

2   Goran, the Human   10

3   The Golden String   18

4   Emil, the Halovit   25

5   The Seventh Bridge   33

6   Yaga, Yaga and Yaga   45

7   The Strawberry Cave   57

8   The Old Salt Mine   69

9   Day of the Kukeri   82

10   The Offer   93

11   The Dream   105

12   The Snowdrop Forest   114

13   The God of the Underworld   122

Epilogue   132

CHAPTER 1

VODNIK

The Great Vodnik of the Eastern Marshlands saw something fall in the water. He was sitting on a rock, half-submerged in a shallow river. It was a stormy night—rain, wind, thunder, lightning—and it had been going on and on for hours. Contrary to what some believed, Vodnik did not like that kind of weather. True, lakes, ponds, and rivers were his home, and he liked being wet more than anything, but weather like this usually kept his potential victims far from his reach. Tonight, he was extremely bored.

Normally, when he was not busy drowning his victims and extracting and preserving their souls in special jars, he was entertaining himself by playing cards with his daughter, Morna. Not tonight.

That was why, when he saw something fall in the river, Vodnik jumped with excitement and quickly dove in to check what it was. His excitement grew stronger when he realized that the thing, whatever it was, was still alive—at least for now. Probably an animal, judging by its size. It would not be as useful as a giant, but it was better than nothing—at least it would break the monotony of the long night. Giants, known as ispolins, were not easy to drown, but they made the finest keep-in-a-jar souls.

Vodnik took his time swimming toward the creature. He liked watching his victims drown. There was something amusing in their futile attempts to reach the surface for a so-needed breath of air. But the highlight was when he got to witness their sheer panic the moment they saw him. To them, his presence meant a sure death by drowning. It was almost impossible to escape from Vodnik. Even excellent swimmers had met their end when they dared enter his abode.

On land, Vodnik was a clumsy, green-haired man with frog-like feet and hands. Water was always dripping from his clothes, which were covered with pond weeds and algae. But in the water, he was at home. Even fish felt obligated to serve him, as he often used them as a quicker and more enjoyable form of transportation.

Suddenly, Vodnik noticed that whatever fell in the water was swimming pretty well and was soon about to reach the river bank and escape. He could not allow that. Breakfast was a few hours away and he could never be sure if something else would come around later. Of course, he could always eat fish, but diversifying his diet whenever possible was always a good idea. Time to check on the swimming creature. With a few strong strokes he came close to it, grabbed it by its legs, and dragged it under the water.

Stamat, the dwarf swimming in the water, was taken by surprise. He had almost reached the land when something grabbed him by the leg. Thrashing and kicking in the water, he came face to face with Vodnik. Vodnik saw Stamat's face, screamed in shock, lifted him up over the water, and threw him onto the riverbank.

"What...what..." Stamat uttered, confused and shaken while trying to catch his breath and get on his feet.

"Are you what I think you are? A dwarf? But how is it possible? I thought you are all dead!" cried Vodnik, jumping around with excitement and rubbing his palms together. "Where are my manners! Let me help you up! Here, here. Sorry for almost drowning you! Oh, boy, this night is getting better and better! What is your name? Where did you fall from? Do you play cards? Oh, no, never mind. It's still too wet out to play cards."

Stamat did not have time to panic at the sight of Vodnik. In theory, he knew the creature very well. Although dwarfs were very skilled swimmers, Stamat and his father, Veehar, had learned to stay away from Vodnik very successfully throughout the years.

But now, Stamat was face to face with Vodnik—and Vodnik's reaction was not what Stamat expected.

"You are not going to drag me back in the river and drown me?" asked Stamat, who decided to grab the bull by the horns.

"What! To drown a dwarf? After I thought I would never see one? Never! Where did you come from anyway?

"I just fell off Lamya's back. A few of us were flying on her back, and she flew into some tall trees and lost control. I have to find my father and my friends—two ispolins and a samodiva. Have you seen any of them?"

"No, I haven't. To be honest with you, I would have

drowned the ispolins. The samodiva—I stay away from them. Very sneaky creatures and excellent swimmers. You never know what to expect of them. Don't tell me—flying on Lamya's back was her idea."

"It was," said Stamat.

"Listen," said Vodnik, "I'll make a deal with you. I'll help you look for your friends and your father if you agree to play cards with me once the storm is over."

"Deal," said Stamat, knowing he had no choice.

Stamat and Vodnik started searching the river. There was no trace of Stamat's companions, but he was sure they were still alive. The river was not too deep and they would have at least found the ispolins—the giants could not be easily missed. He was sure his father was looking for him, too, and must be heartbroken, thinking the worst. But where was he? Where was he searching for him? Or maybe he had decided Stamat could not have survived the fall and had given up. A couple of hours later, they came across Lamya, who was lying lifelessly in the mud. Although she appeared dead, they did not dare approach her.

Finally, shortly before dawn, they abandoned the search. The storm had died out. Stamat was exhausted but could not afford to rest. He had to finish his journey to the Mountain of Perun—his initial destination—and, hopefully, catch up to his companions.

He kept his promise to Vodnik, and at the break of dawn, they played a game of cards. As Vodnik explained, he tried befriending an ispolin once and got him interested in playing cards, but it did not work out. "Ispolins," explained Vodnik, "are not very smart. I drowned him in the end."

Vodnik seemed to enjoy Stamat's company and kept on asking him about his life, his father, and his friends. Stamat's answers were long and detailed enough to satisfy Vodnik's curiosity but vague enough not to reveal his and his father's plans. When Stamat told him about Goran and his quest to find and bring to God Perun three golden apples, Vodnik exclaimed, "Three golden apples? But God Perun can get them himself anytime."

"He can," answered Stamat. "That's why we think this is a test for the ispolins, a test that will determine if they will live or die. They got the apples, but they still have to get to the God's Eye lake up in the Mountain of Perun. If they don't succeed, we might all be in danger."

"You don't say!" said Vodnik, "You'd better go, then. Who knows, they might need you."

Stamat knew he had to follow the river for a few hours before reaching the Mountain of Perun. The ground was still soft from the rain the previous night, and Stamat was not advancing as fast as he hoped to. Left by himself, he knew he was not maintaining his maximum pace as exhaustion and hunger were settling in.

It was well into the afternoon the following day when Stamat reached the bottom of the Mountain of Perun. There were still a few hours of steady climb left. Even if he missed the meeting with God Perun, he was still going to climb up to God's Eye lake and look for his father. He and Veehar had a meeting place—a dry hole chiseled out of the side of a hill—where they would wait for each other in case they got separated. Since they were traveling a lot, they did not use it often. It occurred to him that Veehar might be so sure of his death that he might not go to the meeting place. Nevertheless, he had to try. He knew he would find his father, one way or another.

Stamat paused and took a deep breath. Nothing bad had happened so far. The sun was shining, the birds were chirping—the world around him looked peaceful. The ispolins probably succeeded...

Just then, he felt a strong burst of wind. Stamat ran to the nearby woods. By the time he reached the trees, the sky was covered by an enormous black cloud. Soon after, there was lightning, and thunder so loud that he felt the sound penetrating every cell of his body, the vibration almost tearing him apart. His heart raced, and he hit the ground and passed out in an instant.

***

The deafening thunder woke up Lamya, a ferocious, three-headed green she-dragon, who was lying on the ground unconscious after a very painful fall the previous night. She looked around and immediately felt a sense of urgency. There was nobody around. The she-dragon spread her wings and flapped them a few times to make sure they worked. Then, without hesitation, she took off and sped off toward the great Mountain of Perun.

Soon, she reached God's Eye lake and descended, landing on a group of dead eagles. After morphing into her half-woman half-snake body, she looked around, completely stunned from the destruction around her and from the fact she could not remember anything from the time she left her cave, directed by God Veles to find and kill two ispolins and a samodiva. She had a nagging suspicion that either God Veles or the samodiva had something to do with her memory loss. On the other hand, the samodiva and the ispolins could not have survived an encounter with her. So, it must have been God Veles.

Suddenly, she heard someone whisper her name. She looked around but the only creatures around were birds—injured or dead. Just when she decided her ears were playing a trick on her, the voice spoke again, "Lamya...Lamya..." It was a very soft voice, hardly audible, but this time she was sure she heard it. Who could be talking to her? One of the injured birds, perhaps. "Don't be silly!" she thought, "Birds can't talk!"

"Down here," she heard the voice again. Lamya looked down. There was no one on the ground who could have said that. There were only birds, and a dead snake. "The snake," said the voice, "it's me, God Veles. Help me!"

"Veles! My love, what happened?" exclaimed Lamya. She grabbed what looked like a dead snake. "But that's only half of you!"

"Don't worry about this now!" said God Veles spitefully, "Get me out of here—to your cave, the closest one!"

Lamya took the snake carefully in her hands and kissed it. God Veles felt such gratitude that before he could stop himself, he heard himself saying, "Lamya, help me out this time, and I will never forget it! I will reward you beyond your dreams! One day you will rule this world by my side! Remember that!"

"Oh, Vel," said Lamya fondly, "I love you!"

"Yes," said God Veles impatiently, "now let's get out of here!"

Even cut in half, God Veles still inspired fear and veneration. Without waiting for further command, Lamya lifted her upper body up, turned into a she-dragon, and took off, holding the god of the Underworld gently in her claws.

***

By the time Stamat regained consciousness, it was almost dark. He decided to stay where he was. There was no sense in walking through the night and risking getting lost or worse. Did God Perun kill off the ispolins with his thunder a few hours ago? It seemed quite possible. Lucky for Stamat, he could not think about it too much. Exhaustion took over and within minutes he fell into a deep sleep.

He woke up the next morning and started his climb to God's Eye lake. Hours later, he reached the lake and his fears were confirmed—the area around the lake was unrecognizable. It looked like God Perun met his father and his companions there, but something went wrong. Without wasting more time, Stamat went to his underground hut, a short distance away from the lake, only to find it empty.

He sat down on the ground on a small stump, and for the first time in his life he felt truly tired. His body was exhausted; he could hardly move his legs from the big climb the previous day. This would pass, he thought. What he felt would never go away were the defeat and desperation that had already settled in. He did not have a plan, nor was he thinking of one. It was over. He thought he would be upset and maybe break down and cry, but he did not expect to feel numb and even relieved. All he wanted was to stay where he was, stare at the smoldering pile of bird flesh, and not move for days on end. He avoided thinking about his father. Theoretically, Veehar might still be alive, and until he found proof to the contrary, he would believe just that.

Suddenly, he noticed something glistening next to the pile of dead birds, but he thought the sunlight was playing tricks on his eyes. Hours passed, but the little light spot was still there. It did not matter, whatever it was. He could not bring himself to get up and check on it. Another couple of hours passed and Stamat had to get up and relieve himself. Since he was up anyway, he walked closer to the pile of dead birds and realized what the small shining thing was—a golden apple. He picked it up and placed it in the inside pocket of his vest. Now, he had something to remember that failed quest by, other than the likely loss of his father and the annihilation of all the ispolin kind.

CHAPTER 2
GORAN, THE HUMAN

After leaving God's Eye lake, Goran returned to his village. The first few days he hardly left his hut. He was thrown into a new world and was trying to learn more about it before venturing outside. He observed his neighbors from behind his windows, which made some of them quite uncomfortable. Soon, he started to wonder why God Perun wanted him to remember what happened at God's Eye lake and yet left the rest of the ispolins unaware. They woke up the following morning, and none of them realized how much they had changed overnight. They did not even notice their homes looked bigger now that they had become smaller.

The humans were nicer than ispolins, Goran had to admit. No one had insulted him yet, not that he had given them much of a chance. After the third day of his self-confinement, Goran decided to leave his hut and talk to someone.

"Good morning, Peter," he greeted one of his neighbors. The man was wearing a white cotton shirt tucked in black breeches and fastened with a red, wide girdle around his waist. A black fur hat and black pattens complemented his outfit. He was carrying a capped wooden keg on his shoulder, which seemed quite heavy.

"It is, isn't it, Goran! We haven't seen you all summer. Where have you been?"

"Visited a distant cousin of mine by the Black Sea coast," said Goran quickly as he was expecting the question and had his answer ready.

"It must have been a long trip," said Peter. "Did you ride in a wagon?"

"No," said Goran, "but I rode on Lamya's back on my way home."

"Whose back?" asked Peter.

"Lamya's," repeated Goran.

"Who is Lamya?" asked Peter as he stopped walking, put the keg down on the ground and stared at Goran.

"Lamya—you know, the three-headed dragon."

Peter looked like he wanted to take off but did not want to leave his barrel behind.

"Just kidding," said Goran. He did not want to lose him too soon. "Lamya is a horse. I borrowed it from my cousin."

"Oh," said Peter, seemingly relieved. They continued their walk.

"Where are you headed to?" asked Goran.

"The annual brandy brewing, down by the river. You are not doing it this year?" asked Peter.

"No. You know, I wasn't around all summer. Don't have the grape juice ready."

"I'll tell you what," said Peter, "I will give you a couple of bottles from my brandy, once it's done."

"Really?" said Goran, surprised. "Thank you, Peter!"

"Don't mention it! This way. I will show you a shortcut," said Peter as he pointed at a path through a small blackberry field.

"We just recently cleared this path," explained Peter, "I don't know why we never went this way before..."

"You are going through the blackberry bushes?" exclaimed Goran. "Aren't you afraid?"

"Well, you have to be careful not to step on a snake, but it saves a lot of time," explained Peter.

"No, I meant, aren't you afraid you might get caught and entangled?"

"In the blackberry bush?" said Peter and stopped walking again. "If that happens, I would just disentangle myself. It's not like the bush would actually wrap around my ankle and not let go."

"It used to do that," said Goran quietly.

"It used to do what?"

"It used to be able to kill us!"

"The blackberry bush?"

"Yes!"

The keg was too heavy for Peter to run with. He threw it on the ground and took off, as fast as he could. Goran picked up the keg and continued his walk toward the river.

When he got there, he found a few of his countrymen gathered around a big distillation cauldron placed over a fire. The copper cauldron was half full, but soon it would be filled to the top, as more and more people arrived and poured their grape juice in it. A short, stout man was keeping the fire going and occasionally stirred up the juice with a big wooden stick. Once full, he would put the cauldron lid back on. The lid had a special pipe attached to it. The vapors from the juice would turn into liquid, which would travel slowly through the pipe, reach its end, and drip into a barrel.

Goran noticed Peter standing to the side and talking animatedly to everyone who was willing to listen. He stopped as soon as he saw Goran. All eyes landed on Goran but nobody spoke. Goran approached the cauldron slowly and poured the content of Peter's keg in it.

"You forgot your keg, Peter," he said, "I won't need any bottles of brandy after all. It turns out that I won't be around for the winter, either."

***

Goran left his village. He vowed to find Stamat, the only person, who would remember the ispolins and whom he could tell exactly what happened at God's Eye lake.

Goran did not have a plan. He was sure he would not find Stamat in the area they crashed in while riding on Lamya's back. If Stamat had survived the fall, and Goran had no reason to doubt God Perun's words, he would have tried to reach God's Eye lake as soon as possible and join his father. He would have seen the destruction and thought that no one had survived. Goran wished he had stuck around for a few more days instead of rushing back to his village. He could have found Stamat or Stamat could have found him. Now he had no idea where to look for him. Then, it occurred to him that Stamat might try to find him in his village. Maybe he should have stayed put for a while.

He remembered God Perun's words: "All magical beings are still here, but now, if you want to find them, you will have to search very hard." Goran felt he had no choice. He thought of the only creature who could help him find Stamat—an old woman who traveled around in her flying mortar, who covered great distances and saw things that humans, grounded to the surface of the earth would never see and know. Her name was Baba Yaga. It was true, she could be temperamental, egocentric, and downright dangerous, depending on which of the three Yaga sisters one came across.

Goran found her once, in the previous spring, when he had just started his quest to find the Tree with the golden apples. He would try to retrace his steps, to remember all the places he walked by. He hoped winter would not come early this year as the snow would alter the landscape and make it unrecognizable.

Although this time his journey was very different in its purpose from the first one, he felt like he was doing the quest all over again. The same paths, the same landmarks. This time he kept on reminding himself to keep his eyes open and be careful not to step on a snake.

He was approaching the spot where last spring he first saw Yaga flying, chased by Hala—a she-demon who looked like a black vortex cloud and brought strong wind and hail storms on unsuspecting villages. But this time everything was quiet. Only from time to time a soft burst of wind swirled through the carpet of dead leaves covering the ground.

Suddenly, Goran sensed that someone was following him. He stopped and turned around. He did not see anybody but thought he heard a rustling sound somewhere behind the nearby trees. He continued his walk but tried to step quietly. A few minutes later, he heard the sound again. This time the rustling was louder. He turned around just in time to see a big animal disappear among the thickly settled trees. *Probably a bear*, Goran thought. He kept on looking in the same direction but whatever it was, it had vanished.

Goran realized he felt much vulnerable now that he was not a giant any more. He was thinking of the approaching night and how to find a safe and dry place. He regretted his decision to leave his village so suddenly. He could have at least bought a dagger. A few minutes later, he saw a long, solid branch on the side of the road. He stripped off the twigs and leaves and turned it into a walking stick— and possibly a weapon. That gave him an idea. He should build a fire to keep himself warm and protected for the night. He longingly thought of the time he was an ispolin and never felt afraid of anything but a blackberry bush.

Suddenly, Goran heard the rustling sound again, this time very closely, and a moment later he saw a horse walking slowly in the forest, off the path, almost parallel to him. It seemed like the horse was not following him but trying to walk with him. Goran sped up. The horse sped up too. "Maybe, I should try riding it," thought Goran.

"Come here!" called Goran. The horse got on the path and stopped in front of Goran. A strong smell hit Goran—a smell of swamp, fish and rotting plants. Goran stopped himself just in time not the touch the horse, and yelled, "Shoo! Shoo! Get out of here!"

But the horse did not go away. He reared and tried to topple Goran to the ground. Goran started running, left the path, and dashed through the woods, still holding his stick in his hand. After a while, when he could no longer hear the hoofs behind him, he slowed down and leaned against one of the trees, panting heavily.

"Hello, there!" said Vodnik, who appeared in front of Goran just when the latter was trying to catch his breath, which made this task much more challenging.

To Goran's relief, the stranger looked nothing like God Veles. The creature was covered in green pond weeds, and water dripped from his clothes. Goran had never seen him before, but something was telling him he should not trust the stranger's frog-like smile. So much for magical creatures not easily found these days!

"Good afternoon! Who are you?" asked Goran.

"I am the Great Vodnik of the Eastern Marshlands. And who are you? You are a strange creature! You look like an ispolin but you are much smaller!" said Vodnik, visibly excited.

"I am Goran. Ispolins are no more," said Goran. "We are all humans now. We are smaller, but we are supposed to be better."

"Interesting! Can you swim?" asked Vodnik.

"No idea!" said Goran. "This transformation happened just recently, but I am the only one who remembers it. Long story."

"Can you play cards?" asked Vodnik.

"I never really—"

"Here. I will show you. It's not too hard," said Vodnik enthusiastically.

"I can't. I have to go back to the path. A horse was chasing me, but I think it's gone now!"

"What was wrong with the horse?" asked Vodnik.

"Well, it smelled as if it died, spent some time in a swamp, and came back to life. Did you see it?"

"The smell never bothered the ispolins before," muttered Vodnik.

"What was that?" said Goran.

"Never mind. I have to go!" said Vodnik, and he left as quickly as he had appeared. Armed with this new information, he needed to be alone for a while. He needed time to think. He had to re-evaluate his tactics for alluring humans to his river. For better or for worse, ispolins were no more.

Goran could not sincerely say that he would miss his new acquaintance.

CHAPTER 3
THE GOLDEN STRING

After the epic battle with God Veles, God Perun retreated to his palace—the invisible Tree of Life. The Tree was, without a doubt, fit for a supreme god. Located not far from God's Eye lake, its huge, round trunk towered over the earth, its branches reached high in the heavens, and its roots touched the upper realms of the Underworld. For the time being, the Underworld was without its master, but it looked like everything was going smoothly. It was not such a bad place, after all. It was cool, wet and bustling with dark green vegetation, much like an eternal spring. After his defeat by God Perun, God Veles, the ruler of the Underworld, was left with nothing but his snake body, in fact half of it, as it was severed by a dying eagle only a moment before the bird took its final breath.

With a swift motion of his hand, God Perun lifted all golden apples embedded in the walls of his palace. One by one, they landed in the golden bowl in front of him and immediately started to melt. After the last golden apple melted, God Perun reached inside the bowl with his forefinger and started pulling the substance out, forming a thin, golden string as it was cooling down. After the entire amount of the magma-like matter was extracted from the bowl, he held the string carefully in front of his eyes and examined it closely. The golden apples—the ultimate weapons, the only weapons that could kill a god—were gone. The golden string was the only tool he needed. Very carefully, he placed the string in a jar, closed the lid, and tucked the jar under his belt. Then he summoned his chariot. It was time to retire to his home under the Black Sea and indulge in his newly-found hobby.

***

As God Perun was flying toward the Black Sea coast in his chariot pulled by a pair of bulls, his sworn enemy, God Veles, was resting in a cave and waiting for Lamya to return from hunting, and feed him. He depended entirely on her. He was grateful, of course, that she found him and was taking good care of him. But he was humiliated and helpless, and his desire for vengeance was growing stronger with every passing day.

He had to be patient. He was stuck in his serpentine shape, and until he healed and re-generated the missing part of his body, he would not be able to resume his divine form. In his opinion, it was very unfair for a god to have to endure all this. But at least the snake lived. A normal snake severed in half would have certainly died.

Lamya arrived at the cave carrying a couple of dead geese in her hands, which, strangely, God Veles did not notice. Lately, she spent more time in her snake-like appearance—a long, powerful snake from the waist down and a beautiful, dark-haired woman from the waist up. When hunting, however, she would turn into a three-

19

headed, green she-dragon.

God Veles barked, "What took you so long? I hate waiting!"

"Please, forgive me, my love! I returned as soon as I could."

"Have you been vandalizing ispolin villages again?"

"I tried, my love, but something happened to the ispolins. They are smaller now, deaf and blind."

"What are you talking about? What kind of nonsense is that! If you think this entertains me, it doesn't! Now, chop the mice for me before I starve!"

"I have something better for you, my love. As I said before, the ispolins are deaf and blind. They didn't hear me screeching as I was flying over their villages; they didn't see me descending over their heads as I was ready to attack them. That sucked all the fun out of it! But then I saw a flock of geese wandering around on a narrow street and grabbed two of them for you. Here you are!"

Lamya threw the dead birds on the ground a couple of inches away from Veles's face. Caught by surprise, the snake hissed loudly and angrily, and started writhing his incapacitated body in an attempt to get away from the birds. The expression of excited anticipation on Lamya's face quickly turned to confusion and then fear. Whatever she had done, God Veles did not like, and he would make her pay dearly for it.

"Get these birds away from me!" God Veles bellowed as he managed to regain self-control and stop wriggling. "Have I ever ordered you to bring me birds? I hate birds! I hate looking at them, I hate eating them! Get them out of the cave!"

As Lamya was gliding hastily toward the cave exit, the two geese in hand, God Veles had an extremely unpleasant flashback of his encounter with the eagle that almost ended his life a month earlier.

As soon as Lamya returned, he said to her, "You still have to get my dinner. This time I am coming with you. I'll coil around your claw. I want to see for myself what you are talking about. I bet nothing has changed, but that you have completely lost your mind. Let's go!"

Lamya did not wait to be asked twice. She hurried out of the cave again and once she was out in the open, she lifted up her body as high as she could, turned into a she-dragon, and took off. This time the god of the Underworld was flying with her, safely wrapped around her left claw, observing the world from above once again. Before he could sink into his usual state of self-pity, he reminded himself that one day, in the not so distant future, he would be able to soar in the skies once again, all by himself, in no need of anybody else.

They flew over a dense pine tree forest and then over a large grass field. Soon, the relief became steeper and they reached wooded hills with vertical rocky outcrop—a century-old home of golden eagles. Further down the valley they passed over a small vineyard with some grapes still peeking through its withering leaves. He knew the village could not be too far away.

God Veles almost lost his grip as he took in the changes below. What used to be muddy, often dead-end paths were now narrow cobblestone streets. Someone had reinforced the timber huts with brick and stone, and covered the roofs with tile. But the ispolins, who were walking the streets, looked different—shorter, faster, but definitely not blind or deaf. He saw two women walking together, each carrying a milkmaid's yoke over her shoulder with two copper buckets full of water, one suspended from each end. They were laughing and chatting animatedly. God Perun must have killed off the ispolins! But how did he do it? Veles did not remember a large explosion or a catastrophic event taking place after their fight.

Lamya sped up and with a horrific screech tried to knock down the two women. One of them tripped and fell on the ground, spilling most of the water in her buckets. She got up, and they both looked around, then up—straight through Lamya. One of them said, "How strange! What was that?"

"Must have been a protruding cobblestone," said the other one. "Happens to me all the time!"

Now God Veles knew exactly what Lamya was talking about.

***

The next morning Goran got up early, put out the small fire he had built the previous night, and resumed his walk. He should be reaching Baba Yaga's hut soon. However, after a while he realized he had no idea where it was. The last time he had walked in these woods, he found it by accident. He had not paying attention where he was going then, either, as he had been too distracted by his encounter with Hala, who had just dumped a wall of hail on him.

Goran walked all day, and when the sun started to set, he was sure he had passed the right location and gone too far. He remembered the hut was off a big clearing, but he did not see any on either side of the road. He decided to go back and search more thoroughly. A couple of hours passed as he had searched in vain. It was getting dark, and he decided to give up for the night and find shelter.

Strong winds woke up Goran early the following morning. Heavy drops of cold autumn rain were streaming down his back. The fire he had put together the previous night had died out. He turned on his back and remained lying on the wet ground, looking up the gray cloudy sky. Everything around him was silent and only the wind was whistling through the almost naked trees. He let the rain run down his face for a while.

"Who am I?" he whispered. "Where am I going?"

Goran finally admitted to himself he missed his life as an ispolin, even though he did not like the way it was going most of the time. But he had someone to blame for his misery back then. Now, he was alone. And it was no one's fault that on that cold, windy morning he was looking for a quirky old witch who for some reason now took extra measures not to be found. He was supposed to be different. Better than an ispolin. Instead, he already made too many mistakes. It seemed like with every step, he was lowering the odds of finding Stamat. What would his friends do—the friends he had lost so that he could become a human? Well, at least he knew Stamat's father would never rest until he had found his son.

As if to add to his misery, the rain soon turned into a

downpour and not long after, lightning flashed at the distance. Goran got up, picked up his walking stick and started walking away from the path, deeper and deeper into the forest. He had run out of ideas; he only hoped that sooner or later he would come across Baba Yaga's home—the Hut Standing on One Bird's Leg.

Most of the ispolins who had met Baba Yaga ended up dead with their skulls turned into lanterns, illuminating the grounds surrounding her hut. She was not on good terms with anybody, but particularly despised ispolins and never forgave those who dared making fun of her. She had a reputation of being an evil witch, but this did not deter some ispolins from mocking and teasing her, particularly about her big crooked nose. But they soon regretted it. She would lure them to her hut and feed them the most delicious mushroom soup they had ever had. And the deadliest one.

The poison would not kill them right away. It would work unnoticed for a few hours, effectively destroying their livers and kidneys. Then, just when they were well on their way home, in a good mood and thinking about how they had outsmarted the old hag, they would fall violently sick. Most of them would die in agony within days, with Baba Yaga checking on their progress frequently. She would entertain herself by making small cheerful circles above their huts in her mortar and laughing hysterically. Another skull to add to her precious lantern collection!

The rest of the ispolins avoided her the best they could. Except for Emil.

CHAPTER 4

EMIL, THE HALOVIT

Emil's hut was standing hidden deep in the woods, lonely and dilapidated. No one had ever visited it nor had they knew it existed—except for the woman who had raised him since he was a young boy.

Before Baba Yaga found Emil, lost and crying one cold winter day, she had never thought she would bring an ispolin to her hut. Not alive, anyway. But when the little ispolin stretched out his arms toward her and Yaga did not see fear or disgust in his eyes, she was caught unprepared. And before she knew it, she was carrying him away from the icy river and into her warm hut. She raised him as her own, and all was well until one day they came across Hala. That was how he became a *halovit.*

For years Hala had been trying to catch Yaga off guard and blow her cold deadly breath down Yaga's neck, which would either kill her immediately or make her insane. Finally, one summer afternoon, while hovering over the area as a black vortex cloud, she saw Yaga and the already grown-up Emil in the forest below. She quickly dumped a big hail storm on them. Then, she tried to reach Yaga's neck, but Emil got in the way, protecting her.

This angered Hala. She took a deep breath and blew down Emil's neck instead. Strong chill spread throughout his body. It was not long before he became a halovit and acquired some of Hala's powers. When the weather was nice, he would not feel differently. But when a storm was about to approach, he would fall into a trance and lose consciousness, and his spirit would fly up in the sky, summoning stormy clouds over the neighboring villages.

***

Goran had been walking for a couple of hours when he got the feeling he was moving in circles. The rain and the dark clouds made the visibility worse. He tried to climb on one of the trees to take a look at the surrounding area, but the tree was too slippery, and soon he gave up. He kept on going, driven by pure stubbornness. Suddenly, he saw a small black vortex ascending to the sky. He ran toward a denser part of the forest, not losing eye contact with the vortex. He was sure he saw Hala and knew he had to keep his back and neck covered.

But as he was taking shelter by a big oak tree, he saw the small vortex moving up and further away from him. Clearly, Hala was not interested in him today. He resumed his walk and soon found himself walking toward the area where he had seen the vortex.

He saw the hut, and although it was not the hut he was looking for, his heart jumped with excitement. He recognized it at once. Only one person would dare build their home in Baba Yaga's territory—her adopted son Emil.

Goran recalled the story about Emil he heard last summer

from Yaga's servant, Kikimora. Goran peeked through the cracked window. As far as he could see, there was no one inside. He knocked on the door and when nobody answered, he slowly opened it. The door squeaked loudly in protest. Goran entered the hut but stopped abruptly. A young man was lying on the floor on his back, motionless. Was he asleep? Unconscious? Dead?

Goran approached him carefully and kneeled down next to him. Emil's breathing was regular but faint. His mouth was covered with foam. Suddenly, it became clear to Goran that the small vortex cloud that he saw earlier was not Hala—it was Emil's spirit that had just left his body and was now summoning stormy clouds to the nearby village.

Goran had no choice but to wait for Emil's spirit to return. He looked around. The hut was small, barely furnished but clean. The furniture consisted of a bed, a couple of chairs, and a big working bench, which also served as a dining table. A few baskets weaved out of willow shoots were placed in a corner. Goran picked up one and examined it. It had a handle and a lid. Elaborate multi-colored shapes decorated its side walls. Unlike the baskets he had seen before, the base on that one was not made out of wood but was instead woven out of willow shoots in an intricate pattern. Emil was quite the basket-weaver.

Goran put it down and turned around just in time to see Emil ready to deliver a powerful blow to his head with the mace, which Goran had seen hanging on the wall earlier. Instinctively, he covered his head with his hands and in the process ducked down in time to prevent what would have been a deadly hit.

Goran yelled and dashed toward the table. Emil ran after him fast and tried to reach him with a second blow, but Goran was already at a safe distance on the other side of the table.

"What in the Underworld are you doing! Stop! I just want to talk to you, Emil! Stop!" shouted Goran.

"How do you know my name?" screamed Emil. He stopped chasing the intruder but was still holding the mace above his head, ready to strike.

"I was at Baba Yaga's hut, the Hut Standing on One Bird's Leg, last summer and Kikimora told me all about you," spit out Goran quickly.

"Liar!" shouted Emil and started chasing Goran again, "No ispolin has survived an encounter with Yaga!"

Goran ran around the table and tripped on one of the chairs. He grabbed it to regain his balance, but meanwhile Emil had almost caught up with him. Still holding the chair, Goran lifted it up, turned around and slammed it with all his strength on Emil's head. This caught Emil unprepared. He collapsed on the floor but quickly reached the edge of the table and tried to pull himself up. Goran saw this, overturned the table on the top of Emil, and jumped on it. Emil screamed in pain.

"Sorry, Emil! Just playing it safe! Now listen to me! I helped Baba Yaga when she was running from Hala one night last summer. That's why she spared my life and offered me food and shelter instead. I spent that night in her hut, where I met Kikimora, who told me all about you. How Yaga found you one winter day when you were a little boy wandering around alone and scared, how she raised you, how you became halovit when you saved her life from Hala, and how Yaga has been trying to get hold of Hala's dipper ever since, so that she could exchange it for your sanity."

Emil flinched.

"Don't worry," said Goran, "Your secret is safe with me. Just like you, I don't have any friends. I used to, but they are all gone! Except for one of them, who is lost, and whom I am trying to find. But I need Yaga's help. Can you bring me to her?"

"What does your friend look like?" said Emil quietly.

"He is a dwarf. His name is Stamat."

"I think I know who you are talking about. I haven't seen any other dwarfs around for ages. But I have bad news—he's been taken!"

***

God Perun was sitting in his underwater palace. He pulled out a jar from his robe and looked at the golden string in it. He was quite fond of it. The golden string had exceeded his expectations. When he first got the idea to make a golden string out of all his golden apples, he knew he should be able to create new life forms with it, but he did not expect the results he had been getting. All he needed to do was flick the golden string a little bit differently every time, a little lighter, or a little harder, right in the middle, a little bit to the left, a little bit to the right...in fact, he could not achieve the exact same flick every time, even if he wanted to. He was enjoying himself like never before. With every flick of the string, a new salt water creature appeared—this time a fish, next time a crab, then a sea horse that looked just like a sea weed. Over half a million species and counting!

This morning was not going to be different. He opened the jar and took out the golden string. Then he placed it horizontally at eye level in front of him. It stayed there as if supported by an invisible hand. Flick—a small transparent goby fish appeared as soon as the string stopped vibrating, and swam away. Another flick, and a common dragonet, a pointy little fish, found its way out of the god's palace and into the open water. The following flick produced a long-snouted seahorse. "Oh, how neat!" thought Perun.

Out of nowhere, a thought struck the god of thunder—a very unexpected and quite unpleasant thought. He had just realized that he did not use all golden apples in existence to create the golden string. Two more apples were out there, and he had no idea what happened to them. Two apples lost in the fight with his archenemy, God Veles. The one that God Veles cast at him but was taken by the winds and disappeared. The second one was one of the three apples that Goran had presented to God Perun at the end of the quest. Perun did not use it during the fight, or later on, when he had transformed all ispolins to humans. It got left behind, and was probably still on the ground somewhere by God's Eye lake.

Without further ado, God Perun left the Black Sea, summoned his chariot, and headed straight for the Mountain of Perun. He did not have to do that. All he needed to do was stretch his hand forward and command the apples to fly back to him. He would have had them in his possession within seconds. But something was telling him he should go back to God's Eye lake. He had been avoiding the place for months. It had been a while since the battle, and although he was victorious, he did not want to be reminded of it. That battle had changed everything. God Veles was not just a rival any longer; he was a deadly enemy who would do anything to destroy him.

There was no doubt in God Perun's mind that as soon as God Veles regained his divine form, he would seek vengeance. He was not sure how much time he had until that happened, but he had a feeling it would not be long. Sadly, that meant he had to abandon his hobby for the time being.

As Perun approached God's Eye lake, he saw patches of scorched land. Only the first deep snow would be able to hide the devastation. He landed by God's Eye lake and looked around. He did not expect to see the golden apple but would have no trouble summoning it, along with the other one. He thought about the two apples and stretched his hand. He expected that the one lost at the battlefield would jump to his hand the very next second. The other one might take a minute, depending on which part of the planet it had landed on. Any second now...

But nothing happened. God Perun concentrated again, both hands outstretched. Still nothing. He pictured the two apples in his head for the third time, now slightly panicking. Something was not right. That would only happen if the apples were already in possession of someone else. And God Perun only hoped that that someone was not his archenemy, the god of the Underworld.

CHAPTER 5

THE SEVENTH BRIDGE

"What do you mean, *taken*?" asked Goran.

"Well," said Emil, "my mother told me that her sister, the third Yaga, saw him sitting by the God's Eye lake a couple of weeks ago. The third Yaga was flying around in her mortar looking for something she could cook for dinner. When she saw him, she approached him from above as quietly as she could, grabbed him, threw him in her mortar, and rushed to her hut. My mother said that at first her sister planned on killing and cooking him for dinner, but at the end she changed her mind. You see, my mother and her sisters have a hard time keeping servants. Kikimoras are the only creatures resilient, patient, and desperate enough to put up with them, but even they don't last too long. So the Yaga sisters are always on the lookout for proper help or a slave, if necessary. The dwarf had no choice or he would have been killed. Where are you going?"

"I have to find him. I have wasted too much time. I don't expect that your mother would help me and go against her sister. And you probably won't either. Well, so long."

"Oh, this is where you are wrong. The Yaga sisters love nothing more than to witness each other's misery. When they are together, they tolerate each other, but when they are apart, they can spend days plotting how to make each other's life difficult. And they take it high. Anything short of killing each other is a fair game. But my mother cannot help you tonight. She is visiting her sister. All three are getting together to cook up a potion my mother needs for something, and to talk about what happened to the ispolins. I don't see what the big deal is. We just got a bit shorter, is all."

"You noticed!" exclaimed Goran.

"Of course I noticed! As a start, my hut looks a lot bigger now!" said Emil, wondering why he had to explain something so obvious.

"That's strange. None of the other ispolins notice that. I know about it only because I was there when it happened."

"What are you talking about?" asked Emil.

"It's a long story, and I have to go now. Can you at least point me in the right direction?"

"Yes, keep west and follow the sunset until you reach a vast river that flows southwards. Follow the river but don't cross it. Count the bridges you pass. Once you reach the seventh bridge, cross it, continue straight, and you will soon see the youngest Yaga's hut. I expect you know she is the meanest of the three Yaga sisters. I don't know how you plan on defeating her. That's nearly impossible. And I can't help you because I feel that more stormy weather is on its way, and I have to stay put in my hut. I don't think I will see you alive again, but good luck anyway!" said Emil. He then sat on his bed and stared at a point on the wall.

A minute passed, and Goran realized he was not getting any more information out of Emil. He said thank you and left the hut.

"Wait," yelled Emil a few moments later, "take these."

Goran turned around and saw Emil standing by the door with a lit torch and a small pouch.

"What's in the pouch?" asked Goran.

"Garlic," said Emil. "Keeps dangerous creatures and dark forces away."

"What dangerous creatures?"

"You know, ghouls, bogeys, vampires…You don't know what I am talking about, do you?"

"I do, but I thought those are hard to come across nowadays."

"I don't know who told you that. I never leave my hut without a garlic pouch. Why risk it?" said Emil.

He disappeared inside his hut. Once inside, he opened the big chest sitting by the wall and took out Hala's dipper. He knew his mother was trying to find it. He was glad she was not around today. He would be busy finding a safer place for it. No amount of sanity was worth giving up the feeling of freedom and control he was getting from soaring above the woods, commanding the stormy clouds and winds.

***

That night, Goran did not stop for a rest. He could not fall asleep knowing that Stamat had been captured and enslaved by one of the foulest creatures known in this land. The torch that Emil gave him lasted for about an hour, but Goran had already found the right path. Light rain kept falling throughout the night, but the next morning surprised Goran with clear skies, sunshine, and mild warm breeze. The sunlight, reflected off of the raindrops still covering the trees, made their remaining leaves look even brighter.

Goran was walking as fast as he could. It was noon when he finally arrived at the river and started to follow it to the south. Soon, he reached the first bridge, a small stone structure arching slightly over a shallow part of the river. As Goran passed the bridge, he realized that he would need to come up with a foolproof system to keep track on the bridge count. He could easily see himself walking between the fourth and the fifth bridge and wondering exactly which one he had passed.

He picked up six yellow pine tree needles from the ground. One pine needle for each bridge.

Almost an hour later, he reached the second bridge. It was wooden, very old, and mostly rotten, with more than a few boards missing. "At least I don't have to cross this one," thought Goran and dropped one of the pine needles. Five more to go.

By the time Goran reached the seventh bridge, dusk had already settled in. He was about to sit down and take a rest when it occurred to him that he would have to find Baba Yaga's hut while it was still light. He would keep walking, and hopefully, would notice it from a distance. Once he knew where it was, it would be much easier to find it in the dark later.

This bridge, much bigger than the previous ones, was made

of stone. It was built over a wide part of the river and consisted of two arches. Only a couple of hundred yards upstream, a system of waterfalls caused the otherwise slow river to speed up and churn. Both sides of the river were overgrown with bushes and trees, but since it was late fall, the forest around the river did not seem too dense or impenetrable.

Goran reached the middle of the bridge. He walked to one of the low stone parapets and looked at the surrounding area. His eyes were resting at the mountain in the distance when a sudden movement by the one of the river banks caught his attention. He did not expect to see a stray dog in this part of the woods. The dog saw him too, hesitated, then continued its walk under the bridge. Goran walked to the other parapet, expecting to see the dog reappear, but it was nowhere to be seen. It probably decided that the bridge was a good enough shelter for the night and stayed put.

Goran crossed the bridge and, as Emil had instructed him, continued straight. His steps were muffled by the thick carpet of wet leaves covering the path. He did not have to walk long. Not even half a mile into his walk, he saw smoke rising above the woods on the left side of the path.

He left the trail and carefully made his way through the trees, getting closer and closer to the smoke. Suddenly, someone yelled, "Is it ready, Yaga?" A wave of panic swept over Goran, who did not expect to be so close to the Hut Standing on One Bird's Leg. He threw himself on the ground and froze, trying to listen for the answer.

"Not yet, Yaga. I need you to bring me the boar's horn."

The second voice sounded even closer and Goran realized that whoever asked the question was inside the hut.

"Stamat has it. He's been grinding it for days now!" yelled the first voice.

Goran's heart jumped. Stamat was still alive! Very carefully, hardly able to control his excitement, Goran started crawling in the direction of the voices.

"Hey, you!" yelled the second voice.

Goran froze again. For a second, he thought the voice was talking to him.

"Hey! I am talking to you, dwarf! Come here and bring me the horn powder!"

Goran crawled faster and as soon as he reached a bigger tree, he stopped and slowly got up on his feet, pressing his body against the tree. He peeked out from behind his hiding spot. There was a big round clearing, just a few yards away from him. The Hut Standing on One Bird's Leg was on the opposite end of the clearing. In the middle, there was an unlit fire pit with a big cauldron on the top. Not too far from the fire pit, there was a big metal cage. He saw Stamat walking from the cage toward who he guessed was the second Yaga sister. Stamat's feet were chained together and he was taking his time.

"Finely ground! Just the way I need it!" said the middle sister, looking inside the wooden bowl that Stamat had handed to her. "Where did my sister find you again?"

"Don't bother!" said one of the two Yagas who had just

stepped out of the hut. Goran recognized the oldest sister, so the other one must have been Stamat's master. "He doesn't talk," she added. "He does a good job around the house, but he hasn't said a word ever since I brought him here. He just looks at me with this defiant look. I know he is constantly thinking of ways to escape. Well," she cackled, "he can't!"

Suddenly she stopped, looked up and sniffed the air.

"What is it, Yaga?"

"I smell something. I smell flesh. And it's not shorty over here. It smells like ispolin, but somewhat different."

The three witches started walking in the direction of the woods where Goran was hiding. They had almost reached the end of the clearing. Goran knew it was too late for him to turn around and run. Just as he was wondering if the garlic pouch Emil had given him earlier would be of any help against the Yaga sisters, he heard Stamat saying, "You old hags don't know the ispolins had been wiped out?"

Goran was not sure what stopped them—the fact that Stamat had finally spoken, or the way he spoke to them.

"What do you know about this?" asked the eldest sister.

Goran did not stick around to hear the answer. Taking advantage of the distraction, he lowered himself slowly on the ground, crawled as fast as he could back to the trail and took off. He did not stop running until he reached the big stone bridge and hid underneath it. Goran could not believe his luck. While he waited for darkness to settle in, he started thinking of a plan.

***

Goran was not good in making plans. All he could think of was sneaking back under the cover of darkness and playing it by ear. After a while, when he was sure he was alone, Goran got out of his hiding place, walked back to the middle of the bridge, and sat down on the cold stone, leaning on one of the parapets. It was almost completely dark. The skies were still clear, although the wind had picked up in the past hour.

Suddenly, just as Goran was about to get up and head for the Hut Standing on One Bird's Leg, he heard something odd. A sound that was out of place and time. A sound that at first sounded like the wind howling through the old stones and trees around him. Goran jumped on his feet. And then, he heard it again. This time he knew what it was. Somewhere on that old bridge, miles away from the closest village, hiding in the dark, a woman was crying. She was sobbing softly, but there was something in her voice that made Goran's heart sink. It was a cry of a mourning soul, a cry of someone who had suffered great loss. A cry devout of any hope or consolation.

He looked around. For a moment, he thought he saw a shadow move by the end of the bridge, but when he got there, the shadow had disappeared. The dark river underneath was flowing slowly and quietly. The wind had died down. Goran heard a dog's barking by the opposite side of the bridge. He quickly turned around just in time to see a tall dark-haired woman standing halfway between him and the middle of the bridge. She was dressed in black. Her long hair covered her shoulders down to her waist. She was holding a small object in her hands, but Goran could not tell what it was.

Staring silently at Goran, she twitched her finger, beckoning him forward. Goran knew he did not have time to get involved in this but somehow felt he had no choice. He approached the woman slowly, trying to see her face, but it remained hidden in the shadow.

"I was a young bride," he heard her raspy voice, "My groom was a head mason. On the third day after our wedding he and his workmen started building this bridge. But they couldn't finish it. Every time they came close to done, it would collapse. Finally, the elders of the village said that one of builders, the most experienced one, had to sacrifice what was most precious to him.

"I was immured in the bridge pier underneath. It was a very slow death. They finished the bridge, and it has been standing strong ever since. But not long after that, my husband lost his sanity. The horrible memories were too much for him to bear. He couldn't forgive himself that he had allowed this to happen. One day, he wrapped a big stone around his neck and jumped from this very bridge into the cold waters below."

It was one of those moments when Goran had to do a few things at once, and he never liked that. Still digesting the story, he realized that the woman who was talking to him was a ghost whose face he could still not clearly see and who was holding something he could still not recognize. He was not sure if he should feel sorry for her and offer a word of comfort, or panic and run.

"Have you seen a dog around here?" he asked, "a big gray one."

"I have not, but I know the dog you are speaking of."

"What do you mean?" asked Goran.

"Come along," said the ghost.

Goran did not like the direction this conversation was going, but once again he felt he had no choice.

The ghost led Goran off the bridge and into the woods. "Well, at least I am on the right side of the river," thought Goran.

A few steps into the forest, the ghost stopped by a small clearing and handed him the small object she was holding. It was a wooden spindle.

"What do you want me to do with this?" Goran asked.

"I haven't told you the end of the story. After they pulled my husband's body out of the water, they buried him right here. It was a prompt burial and since he took his own life, his grave was never marked. Unfortunately, not long after that, he turned into a varkolak—a blood-drinking wolf. He roams these woods at night looking for victims to satisfy his thirst, and returns to his grave at dawn. You have to kill him by piercing his heart with this spindle. Then, and only then, he would finally find peace. I would have done it myself, but I am too weak."

"You want me to do what?"

Goran heard a loud rustling sound behind him and turned around just in time to see a big wolf-like creature standing on his powerful hind legs, blood dripping from his jaws. The varkolak leaned slightly forward on his right paw, ready to jump.

"Didn't you say he comes back to his grave at dawn?"

whispered Goran, tightening his grip on the spindle in full realization how useless it was against the strong muscular beast in front of him.

"He has extraordinary hearing. As I expected, he heard us from miles away. Now kill him!"

"How strong do you think I am? How do you expect me to—"

Before he could finish, the varkolak pounced on Goran and knocked him down on the ground like a rag doll. Goran saw the varkolak's huge jaws inches from his face and felt his hot foul breath. He dropped the spindle and instinctively covered his face. For a second, he felt the beast's weight crushing his body and knew it was over. Goran thought about Stamat and how his friend would never know that someone never gave up looking for him.

The varkolak roared and Goran realized the monster was taking too long to kill him. The second howl confirmed Goran's initial suspicion that something was wrong.

The varkolak lifted his body off of Goran and stood on his rear legs. He was roaring in pain and trying to lick his chest. Goran smelled burning fur and flesh. He looked down his own chest. He was not hurt. As the varkolak was running away yelping and whimpering, Goran realized that during the attack the small pouch of garlic must have pressed on the beast's chest, causing him great pain, and saving Goran's life.

Without waiting any longer, Goran jumped on his feet and raced through the forest, congratulating himself for the decision he had made earlier to get himself familiar with the path leading to the

Hut Standing on One Bird's Leg.

The dark-haired ghost picked her spindle up and slowly retrieved to her favorite spot on the bridge. Away from the shadow of the trees, the soft moonlight revealed her gaunt, discolored face and hollow, inconsolable eyes.

CHAPTER 6

YAGA, YAGA AND YAGA

Goran arrived at the Hut Standing on One Bird's Leg out of breath and drenched in sweat. He was standing at the edge of the forest, peeking from behind a big walnut tree. The Yaga sisters were standing around a big copper cauldron placed over the fire pit. It was steaming intensely. They must have found all the ingredients they needed, but judging by their loud animated conversation, something was wrong.

"Check the list again, Yaga!" said the eldest sister, "I still can't see it. You said this recipe worked every time!"

"Already checked, before we even started the fire—we had all the ingredients and we put them all in the cauldron! I think you are just not concentrating hard enough! Let's try this again and this time make sure you do your part right!" snapped the youngest sister. "I will stir the potion this time, we all read the ingredients, and you concentrate very hard! I know this works because it has worked for me before. Remember when I lost my pestle? This is how I found it. It was stolen by some pranksters. Well, their mothers never heard from them again," she chuckled. OK, here we go…"

Seven legs of seven scabby toads,

heart of weasel, tooth of goat.

Tiny pups abandoned in a roost,

head of owl, eyes removed.

Claws of raven, set of four,

finely grinded horn of boar.

Thumb of a deceased

whose corpse was buried,

then undug, and right at midnight,

once again reburied.

And a cat when passing by one eerie night,

jumped over it and scurried out of sight.

The eldest Yaga sister was staring at the concoction visibly upset, trying to see something in it that was missing.

"See," she yelled with frustration, "I can only see the handle, just the handle resting on white background. What is this place? And where is the rest? Where is the rest of the dipper?"

Just then, Stamat heard rustling and looked up. He thought he saw someone standing behind the big walnut tree growing at the edge of the woods, just a few feet from the cage he was locked in but could not tell for sure. Thick gray clouds had covered the moon. He stared at the tree, straining his eyes, wondering if there was someone there, or if his imagination was playing a bad joke on him.

"What is this dipper that you lost anyway?" He was distracted by the middle Yaga's voice. "I've got a couple. If you need one so much, I'll let you borrow one of mine."

"No! I don't need one of yours! I have to find mine!" yelled her sister.

"What's so special about yours?"

"Nothing that concerns you. Let's try one more time! Maybe this time I'll see more than a handle!"

Goran, who, up to that moment, was listening to the conversation, decided it was a good time to get closer to Stamat and get his attention. He dropped down on his knees and elbows and crawled closer to Stamat's cage.

Everyone else, including Stamat, was concentrating on the cauldron.

Seven legs of seven scabby toads,
heart of weasel, tooth of goat...

Goran picked up a small pebble and threw it at Stamat, who jumped, startled, and turned back quickly. Under the feeble light of the fire, just a couple of feet away from him, he could clearly make up Goran's grinning face.

Tiny pups abandoned in a roost,
head of owl, eyes removed...

It took him a second to realize that the face was attached to the rest of Goran, who had somehow found him and had come to his rescue. Before he could stop himself, he let out a loud gasp of surprise.

Goran got down on the ground and quickly hid behind the closest tree only a moment before the three sisters made a dash for the cage. The youngest one was already screaming at Stamat, "What are you doing, you miserable dwarf? How dare you interrupt us!"

Goran was not ready for this turn of events but realized that now he did not have to come up with a plan. He could play it by ear. To his surprise, Stamat started laughing. "He is buying me time," thought Goran, "or maybe trying to cover his excitement…"

"I feel so bad for you amateurs," Stamat said, then burst into peals of laughter before continuing. "Your ignorance is deplorable! You will never get this magic to work! You have it all wrong!"

"What are you talking about, dwarf?" yelled the middle sister, but there was not a trace of confidence in her voice. The rest were looking at him, stunned. "What do you know about this?"

"You are out of your demented minds if you think I would just tell you. Let me out of this cage, and maybe I'll talk!"

"We can't do that! He will escape!" screamed the youngest sister.

"Open the cage, Yaga!" said the oldest one. "He is not going anywhere. Look at him. How fast do you think he can run?"

"If this costs me my slave, Yaga, I will make sure you won't see another day!"

"I am sure you will! Now hand me the key!" said the eldest sister in a tone that indicated the argument was over.

Followed by the three witches and with a slight smirk on his face, Stamat approached the cauldron, grabbed the big spoon out of Yaga's hand and stirred the potion. Then scooped some of it, lifted it up to his nose, smelled it and threw it back in the cauldron with disgust. He repeated this move a few more times while the three witches observed impatiently.

"So?" said the eldest one.

"It doesn't smell right," said Goran. "Something is missing. Was the cat that jumped over the grave black?"

"Yes, it was," said the youngest one confidently.

"Good. Did it jump three times? Facing the grave, did it jump right to left, left to right and right to left again?

"I...I think it did," said the youngest Yaga, but it became clear she was not sure at all.

"I don't think it did!" yelled Stamat at her. "You of all creatures should know the importance of the number three. If that cat didn't jump three times and in the manner I just described, what you have here is completely useless. You might as well throw it away!"

And with that, he knocked the cauldron down, pouring its boiling content all over her legs. The youngest Yaga sister fell on the ground and screamed in agony as the hot liquid was turning her skin into large and extremely painful bubbles. Her two sisters rushed to her help. They tried to remove her socks but the thick woven material had already stuck to her feet. Shaking with pain, she hissed, "Leave me alone and bring this wicked dwarf back to me. I want him alive!"

Stamat ran toward the three mortars left by the Hut Standing on One Bird's Leg. The middle sister picked up a big rock and threw it at him. She almost hit him. Stamat was still running, but they were catching up to him fast.

Goran saw a branch lying on the ground and grabbed it. As he was making his way through the trees, the eldest sister pick up another rock. This time the rock hit Stamat's leg. He stumbled and fell down.

Without waiting any longer, Goran ran out of the woods and jumped between Stamat and his pursuers, waving his stick and yelling. The Yaga sisters froze. This gave Stamat a few extra seconds to recover.

"You!" finally yelled the eldest sister, recognizing Goran. "You! You!"

That was all she could yell, as a result of seeing a smaller version of Goran, seeing him so unexpectedly, and realizing that she could not let her sisters find out that he was once her guest, who left her home alive.

"Do you know him? Who is he? What is he? This is no ispolin!" shrieked the second Yaga.

"No, I don't! Get him!"

"Stop!" yelled Goran, "I wouldn't do this if I were you! Let us go and I won't hurt you! You are right! I am no ispolin! I am a human! You have no idea what we are capable of!"

With the corner of his eye, Goran noticed that Stamat had

almost reached one of the mortars.

"I can cast a spell on you and turn you to whatever I want! Or I can make you disappear!" shouted Goran.

The witches hesitated. Goran was contemplating his next move when a horrific shriek interrupted whatever plan was forming in his head, "Get them, you imbeciles! My slave is getting away!"

"Run!" screamed Stamat.

Goran ran like he had never run before. Stamat was standing by the mortar ready to jump in. Goran had no idea how to drive a mortar, but Stamat seemed pretty confident. He reached the mortar, helped Stamat in, jumped in, and before he could say anything, he heard Stamat yelling, "Og! Pu! Og, og, og!"

The mortar lifted off the ground with a jerk.

"Pu! Pu! Og! Og! Og!"

"What are you saying?" asked Goran. "What does this mean?"

The mortar was already high up in the air. Yelling at each other, the two Yaga sisters were getting into one of the other mortars. Stamat took the pestle and tried to steer the mortar, but the pestle was too heavy for him.

"Here," said Stamat, letting Goran take charge of the pestle, "you handle this, and just use it as a paddle. This model of mortars pretty much does everything for you, so you will hardly need the pestle anyway. They even have a reverse command feature as a protection against theft. You see, instead of *go*, they respond to *og*. Instead of *up*, you have to yell *pu*. If you just say *go* and *up*, it won't move. Pretty neat!"

"Who makes these?" asked Goran.

"Who do you think? Ispolins?" laughed Stamat. "We do. There is an old dwarf family who has been making these for centuries. Who are you?"

"Goran. And please trust me. I will tell you everything that happen if we ever get out of here alive. Is there a way we can speed this up?"

"You are Goran? Where is my father? Is my father alive?"

"I am sorry, Stamat! He is not. Well, not exactly."

"What do you mean not exactly?" screamed Stamat.

"I will tell you everything, but we have to get out of here first!"

"That's what I expected anyway! I knew he was dead," said Stamat quietly.

"Stamat, I am very sorry I had to bring such bad news! But there is more to that."

The mortar swerved into the path heading to the old stone bridge, and Goran tried to steady the pestle. The mortar was picking up speed, but their pursuers were not far behind.

"Give me that!" yelled Stamat as he grabbed the pestle from Goran. In his fury and desperation, he did not feel its weight.

The mortar was flying at top speed when Stamat almost crashed it into a tree and had to make a sharp turn to avoid collision. Goran wondered if Stamat had planned to crash the mortar but had changed his mind in the last moment. With his nerves on edge,

Goran could hardly trust his intuition. Either way, the near crash slowed the mortar down and the Yaga sisters were closing in, as their flight was much smoother.

As Stamat was straightening up the pestle, their mortar took a violent hit from behind. The witches cackled with newly-gained confidence. As they were gaining speed for another collision, Stamat yelled, "Pu, pu, pu! Og pu!"

Their mortar ascended fast and soon reached the top of the highest trees. It hovered for a second and then took off unobstructed.

Goran looked back, but the witches were nowhere to be seen. For the first time that evening, he started to think that he might survive the night after all.

Goran did not expect to see the dark-haired ghost he met earlier still standing on the bridge. She was leaning on one of the stone parapets, gazing at the dark waters underneath. She did not seem to have noticed them.

"Rada," he heard Stamat saying.

"What did you say?" asked Goran.

"Her name was Rada. She is a talasam now, a ghost of someone who has been immured," continued Stamat. "Immured means someone who was left to die embedded in—"

"I know what it means," interrupted Goran, "as I met her earlier. She told me how she died. She also introduced me to her husband, who is now a varkolak on account of killing himself and being buried in an unmarked grave. The only thing that saved me was a pouch of garlic I carry around my neck. How do you know her?"

"My father and I traveled a lot. We spent quite some time in these woods. We met her a few times. Sometimes she would be the dark-haired woman you saw today, and sometimes, usually during the day, she would take the form of a big gray dog."

"She was the dog!" exclaimed Goran. "That's why she told me she knew the dog I was asking her about, but she had never seen it!"

Before Stamat could respond, a violent collision from underneath sent the mortar flying up and almost flipped it upside down. Stamat fell out but managed to grab its edge. While Goran was pulling him back in, they lost control of the mortar, which started to spin and descend fast despite their frantic yells at it to go up. After a few moments, it landed on the old stone bridge, not as softly as the two riders inside would have hoped. The Yaga sisters were right behind them.

The talasam had disappeared. Goran grabbed the pestle. They ran across the bridge, but just as they were about reach the end, the two Yaga sisters landed on the river bank and jumped off their mortar.

The younger witch rushed onto Stamat and knocked him down. She was much taller than him but his stout and muscular body was not easy to overpower. She was trying to pin him down and choke him to death. He was fending her off with punches and kicks.

While the two were wrestling on the ground, Goran and the oldest Yaga were fighting with their pestles. The sound of clashing weapons echoed through the silent forest.

"Listen," whispered Goran while blocking two consecutives blows, "I don't want to hurt you. I wasn't looking for this fight."

"You hurting me!" chuckled Baba Yaga, "I don't think you know who you're dealing with! Anyway, there is no going back now, is there!"

Although smaller than Goran, she was faster, controlled her pestle better, and landed more than a few heavy blows on Goran's body. The last one hit Goran's left knee. He lost balance and fell to the ground. As he was cursing and trying to get back up, he saw the other Yaga pinning Stamat to the ground, her hands viciously squeezing his neck.

"Stamat!" yelled Goran.

The younger Yaga instinctively looked up and loosened her grip on Samat's throat. This was the distraction he was waiting for. He reached into his pocket, pulled out a boar's horn, and stabbed her in the eye with all his remaining strength. A stream of blood splashed Stamat and spilled all over the ground around him. Yaga covered her face and fell on the ground, her whole body convulsing in pain. When in a few seconds she managed to take a breath, her screams made the sleeping forest shudder with horror.

Her sister was standing motionless. Goran was back on his feet. He looked at the oldest Yaga, and it became clear to him that she was not going to fight. Stamat must have sensed that too, because he walked to the water, splashed his face a few times to wash off the blood, went back to the witch still screaming and rolling on the ground in agony, and picked up the boar's horn. He said, "The cat's manner of jumping over the grave didn't really matter. What you were missing was this boar's horn, which I was supposed to grind to dust. Well, I thought, if I just hid it in my pocket instead, it might come in handy someday."

Moments later Goran and Stamat jumped into one of the mortars left on the river bank and took off.

A very pale woman with long dark hair appeared on the bridge and gestured toward the oldest Yaga to approach her.

"Not now, Rada, not now!" blurted Yaga, wondering how the events of that night could have gone downhill so fast, and hardly controlling her desire to unload her fury on the innocent ghostly bystander.

CHAPTER 7

THE STRAWBERRY CAVE

For the first time in years, Goran was glad to be back home. He dusted off the thick layer of dust from the furniture, lit up the small fireplace, brought in a couple of buckets of water from the river over the hill, and prepared a hot potato stew from the basic provisions he kept in his closet.

For the past half hour, neither Goran nor his guest had spoken a word. The potato stew in the two large bowls was quickly disappearing only to be replenished with more from the steaming pot hanging over the fireplace. One of the two loaves of bread placed in the middle of the table was almost gone.

Goran and Stamat were sitting around a short round wooden table. A big wicker-covered demijohn full of red wine was standing on the floor between them.

"So," said Stamat, "where were we? Oh, yeah. As we were flying on that mortar, you started telling me you were Goran, but you were no longer an ispolin. How is that possible?"

Goran watched as the dwarf poured just a small amount of the dark red liquid into a bowl. He hesitated.

"What?" said Stamat as Goran did not respond.

"Keep pouring," said Goran, "It's a long story and I'll tell you now. You won't believe it!"

"Okay," said Stamat, filling up his bowl to the brim, "I have all the time in the world. Give it a try."

"We looked for you," said Goran, "we looked everywhere—up the river, down the river, in the forest around the river, we didn't stop looking for you until the following morning. Your father died that night. Zara was devastated. She couldn't stop crying. She had decided it was her fault, since she was the one who suggested that we flew on Lamya."

"We all agreed on that!" interrupted Stamat.

"That's what we told her, but she didn't want to hear it."

"Is she dead too?"

"If you ask me, your father, Zara, Spas, they all are dead. We won't see them again. If you ask God Perun, they all live on—in me. I kind of died too when he blew us all up with one of the golden apples. But I woke up the following morning as a new creature, a human. I woke up smaller, but smarter, more intelligent and better overall. I had acquired the best of Spas, Zara, and Veehar. At least that's what God Perun told me when I woke up."

"He threw a golden apple at all of you and transformed everyone into one creature—you?" Stamat could not believe his ears.

"Yeah. That's pretty much what happened."

Stamat was silent.

"I want you to know something, Stamat, and I swear I am not making this up just to make you feel better. At one point in our conversation with God Perun, your father threw one of his own golden apples at him. I have no idea how he got that apple. Anyway, as you could imagine, that didn't do much. God Perun caught it effortlessly. But he wasn't angry. Instead, he told Veehar how sorry he was for what he had done to your race. He also told us you were still alive. I looked at your father's face. I had never seen a happier person. And that's how he died. God Perun threw his golden apple at us right after that. Believe me, none of us realized what happened."

Stamat was still silent.

"I believe you," he finally said, "and that's why you came looking for me. You are a true friend, Goran. I never thought I would ever say this to an ispolin, let alone a human!" He chuckled. "So, after all, God Perun did not kill off the ispolins, as I suspected. Instead, he transformed them! On account of my father and our friends!"

"I didn't ask for it, Stamat. You know the story. I was thrown into that quest against my will and with practically no choice. All this time I thought I was saving my race. Instead, it turned out I was leading my friends to their deaths! How could have I predicted that? Even God Perun said he didn't get the idea until we all showed up on the top of the mountain ready to deliver the three golden apples."

"I am not blaming you," said Stamat dryly. "It sounds like you are the one blaming yourself. But one thing is clear to me—God Perun is done killing."

Goran did not respond. He poured himself another bowl of wine. Stamat topped off his. The two drank in silence for quite some time.

Goran was chewing pensively what was left of the bread when, suddenly, Stamat reached into his pocket, pulled out the golden apple he found on the top of the Mountain of Perun and slammed it on the top of the wooden table.

Goran's jaw dropped open as he was about to swallow a piece of bread. A few moments passed while he was wondering if all this could be a nightmare—a nightmare in which he was haunted by golden apples that kept on popping up unexpectedly in the most unusual places. When he finally swallowed his overly soggy piece of bread, it ended up in the wrong pipe. He choked, coughed extensively, threw up some of it back in his mouth, swallowed it again, and hiccupped loudly.

Stamat burst out laughing.

His laughter filled up the small hut, rushed through the narrow cobblestone street, and made a few of the neighbors poke their heads out of their small windows and look around.

"Where do you people get these apples from?" asked Goran. "Do dwarfs grow their own golden apple trees anywhere?"

"Of course not," chuckled Stamat. "I don't know how my father got his. He never showed it to me or mentioned anything about it. He must have taken it from God Perun's palace when we broke in during the last solar eclipse. I found this one when I was still up on the mountain not far from God's Eye lake a couple of days after you got turned into a human. Do you think God Perun is looking for it?"

"I think the more important question is, is God Veles looking for it? Although he was almost killed by God Perun, he would recover sooner or later and I imagine, he would seek revenge. God Perun said that only a golden apple could truly kill a god. Once the gods find it, I wouldn't want to be caught in the middle. Apparently, none of them have found it yet. Either they don't realize this one still exists, or the apple is not easy to locate, even for them. What are you going to do with it?"

"Haven't decided yet. But it would be a good piece of evidence for when I go back to the caves where most of the dwarfs live. I will give it one last try. I will tell them what happened. I will show them the golden apple. If they don't believe me now, if they don't see it's safe to leave the caves, I will leave them alone. But I want to try to finish what my father and I started all these years ago. So long, Goran. Thank you for having my back all this time!"

Stamat headed to the door.

"Stamat," said Goran, "wouldn't they believe you more if they saw the new species God Perun created?"

"Of course, but I don't know how I would convince them to come to one of your villages. Are you saying you want to come with me?"

"Why not? I have already earned a reputation as the village nutcase. Nothing more to do here. We leave first thing in the morning. What do you say?"

"I wouldn't say no to that, Goran. I wouldn't say no."

***

The morning surprised Goran with a heavy blanket of snow. He brought in a few logs from the small shed adjacent to his hut and lit up the fireplace. Stamat was still sleeping. Goran quickly scrambled some eggs with the remaining sheep cheese he had got from the market the day before.

He would be leaving again with no idea if and when he would return. While waiting for Stamat to wake up, he shuffled through his closet and pulled out a couple of heavy wool coats, one bigger than the other. From the back of the closet he retrieved two pairs of fur boots and two fur hats. "It's a good thing I don't throw anything away," he thought.

The smell of scrambled eggs woke up Stamat.

"Morning," said Goran, "the eggs must have cooled down by now. Let's eat."

"It's snowing," noted Stamat, while devouring his breakfast. "We have to use Yaga's mortar again. Otherwise, it would take us weeks to get to the caves."

Goran did not like the idea.

"What if someone sees us?" he said. "Most of the villagers already think I am insane. If they see me flying in this thing, they would think I had become a wizard or something like that. They will start fearing me, and this will not end well. Look at the Yagas. No wonder why they are so mean and short-tempered."

"Nobody will see us. We left the mortar quite a distance from the village, remember?"

They stepped out of the hut and found themselves on a

snow-covered, eerily quiet street. The village had huddled beneath its fresh white cover, and the smoking chimneys were the only telltale sign that its residents had not deserted it. In fact, Goran had a very distinct feeling that a few of his neighbors had glued their noses to their windows wondering what he was up to this time. The feeling that they were being watched did not leave him until they reached the last of the huts.

From there, they walked another mile, until they reached the forest where they had hid the mortar. They removed most of the snow accumulated inside and climbed in. Goran left the flying to Stamat. From time to time, when Stamat had to change direction, Goran helped him to steer the pestle.

The two flew over several small villages, and soon Goran realized his worries were in vain. The snow, which kept on falling steadily was like a veil, which made the mortar and everyone in it invisible to the people on the ground.

They flew southeast, and by noon they reached the Strawberry Cave.

Most dwarfs lived in old abandoned mines, but some preferred natural caves. The Strawberry Cave was the cave Stamat was born and spent most of his life in, before he and his father left it several years ago. Nobody knew why it was called the Strawberry Cave. There were no strawberries growing near it.

When Stamat had been a young boy, his mother talked about how she wanted to leave the cave and start a new life outside in the open. But his parents never made the final move. Maybe they were still too afraid, or maybe there were too many of their neighbors telling them it was a bad idea. It was not before Stamat's mother fell ill and died when Veehar took Stamat outside for good and never looked back.

A few years later, Veehar and Stamat were convinced that there was no more danger of God Perun killing off what was left of the dwarfs. They went back to the cave, but their presence was met with fear and hostility. They tried to talk to the elders, and then to everybody else. Almost nobody wanted to listen, and those of them who showed some interest were quickly silenced by the majority.

That was when Stamat and his father decided to do something drastic and ended up finding and breaking into God Perun's palace and eventually getting involved with Goran and his quest for the golden apples.

Despite years of futile efforts and disappointment, Stamat was ready to go back to his kind and give it one last try. That was what Veehar would have wanted him to do. This time, he was bringing evidence with him: one golden apple and a newly-created human.

Goran and Stamat landed the mortar not far from the cave entrance.

The cave was about six miles long and contained three levels with many intersecting galleries and vast halls. The middle level was the one with a direct connection to the entrance of the cave. They approached the entrance and went inside. The gallery was illuminated by numerous small fires. Goran and Stamat paused to let their eyes get used to the surroundings. They heard someone yell, "Stop right there! Don't move!"

A stout dwarf with a torch in his hand quickly approached them.

"Who are you and what do you want?" he asked, shoving the torch in their faces.

"I am Stamat and this is my friend Goran. I used to live here with my father, Veehar. Please let us in. We need to speak with the elders."

"Hmm. I remember you. What happened to your friend? Why is he so tall?" said the guard, eyeing Goran suspiciously.

"Well, this is why we came here. We would like to meet with the elders first and discuss a very important matter," said Stamat loudly. He was sure that at least one of the elders was snooping around the entrance at any given time and did not want to be accused of ignoring the procedure and not talking to the elders first.

"Stamat!" exclaimed another dwarf who had just materialized in front of them. It was one of the elders.

"Boyan!" said Stamat and bowed.

"It's been a long time," said Boyan, "a very, very long time!"

"Well, not *that* long," said Stamat. "I am not *that* old yet."

Boyan chuckled. "Where is your dad?" he asked.

"He is dead," said Stamat.

"Actually, he is..." Goran started explaining but was interrupted by Boyan who said, "I always knew he would get himself in trouble sooner or later. Such a rebellious spirit. I told him that one day he would get more than he bargained for! Too bad, too bad for him… and you."

"Boyan," said Stamat, "things have changed. That's why we have come here. We want you to know what's going on out in the world. There is no more danger for us. This time I can prove it."

This conversation started attracting other dwarfs, who circled Stamat, Goran, and Boyan. Boyan seemed uneasy.

"Who is your friend?" asked Boyan in an attempt to change the conversation, "and what happened to him? Why is he so tall?"

"This is Goran. And he has quite a story tell you. He is so tall because he is not a dwarf. He is a human."

Boyan immediately regretted asking.

"I need to talk privately with these two newcomers! Everybody, leave the area now! This might be dangerous! Everybody leave! Guards! Guards! Please escort everyone to their parts of the cave!"

"But I know Stamat!" yelled a young dwarf. "He was my neighbor. He was always nice. He was not dangerous!"

"Come along. Let's go. Let's find Neno," said the young dwarf's mother and shoved him away from the entrance and into the upper level of the cave.

After everyone had left, Boyan turned to Stamat and said, "What are you trying to do? What is this nonsense? What do you mean by "human"? Your friend is just a freak of nature and everybody can clearly see that! Why did you come back?" His voice trembled with anger.

"I came back to rescue my people. To rescue them from the prison they have put themselves into. My father and I have tried to do this for years, as you know, unsuccessfully. But this time I have proof! Look at this creature!" Stamat's voice was getting equally angry. "Take a good look! He used to be an ispolin. God Perun didn't like them either. But do you know what he didn't do this time? He didn't wipe them out! He changed them into this half-ispolin half-dwarf creature he called a human. He is done killing his creatures once and for all! Leave the caves! We can start from where we left off centuries ago. We don't have to continue living this way."

"And how do you know this really happened? How do you know God Perun didn't wipe out the ispolins and replace them with humans?" said Boyan.

"Because this human right here used to be an ispolin. I knew him when he was an ispolin. But now he is not. God Perun changed him into a human, and my friend remembers how it happened. And before the transformation God Perun told him how much he regretted what he had done to us. He is done killing! My people need to hear this!"

"So, you're saying that your friend here has talked to God Perun personally?" cried the elder, "Get out of my cave!"

"Well, that was a tremendous waste of time," said Stamat, visibly upset after the guards threw him and Goran back outside.

"No, it wasn't," said Goran, "we learned two important lessons. First, ignore the elders and speak with the rest of the dwarfs first if possible, and second, don't ever mention again that I have spoken with a god. This claim would need a pretty convincing evidence. Let's go."

"Where are we going?"

"To the next cave, of course. This might be Veehar talking now, but if you think I will let you give up now, you are out of your mind!"

***

If Boyan thought that there were no witnesses of his conversation with Stamat and Goran, he was wrong. Little Neno managed to duck down and hide behind one of the bigger stalagmites located nearby. The guards did not see him and neither did his brother and mother, who were looking for him.

After Boyan retreated and the guards resumed their usual absentminded stroll, Neno carefully crawled back to the upper level and joined his family. By that time, his mother was worrying sick, but his father, being the voice of reason, kept on repeating, "He will be back any minute now. It's not like he could have left this cave."

At the sight of Neno, his mother rushed to hug and berate him at the same time, but he stopped her with a gesture and said, "I have to tell you what I just heard—and you won't believe your ears!"

CHAPTER 8

THE OLD SALT MINE

"The Old Salt Mine is just a few hours away from here," said Stamat as they got back to the mortar. "It's huge. It's like an underground settlement—one of the largest in this land. I say let's not waste our time with the smaller locations. We can visit those later."

"I agree," replied Goran. "To the Old Salt Mine!" he yelled at the mortar, which did not move.

"Did you forget," said Stamat impatiently, "that you cannot just say whatever you want. It only responds to basic commands, provided they are said backward. Here, hold the pestle. Og pu! Og pu!" he yelled, and the mortar hovered over the ground for a few seconds and ascended into the snowy skies.

By the time they got to their destination, it was late afternoon. It was still snowing, but the temperature had dropped considerably. Goran and Stamat decided to seek shelter in the salt mine without revealing the real purpose of their visit until the following morning.

The salt mine had been known for many centuries. Dwarfs had been extracting salt and trading it for as long as they could remember. However, in the years after the flood, the operation almost died out. Now only small quantities were obtained and traded in for other necessities, such as meat and fur.

Currency had been hard to come by, so when the guards heard that Goran and Stamat would be paying for the salt with five golden perperos, they became very accommodating. Without asking too many questions, they immediately brought them to two spacious horizontal shafts. That part of the mine was at a comfortable sixty degrees all year round. The shaft floors were covered with thick bear skin. In each shaft there was a low but spacious wooden bed covered with soft blankets as well as pillows filled with goose feathers.

Stamat fell asleep as soon as his head hit the pillow, but Goran did not fall asleep until midnight. He was thinking about the conversation with the dwarfs the following morning. When he finally dozed off, he had a dream that he was walking barefoot on the snow, sprinkling the path in front of him with the salt he was holding in a big wooden bowl.

When Goran woke up the following morning, Stamat was not in his quarters. Goran wandered for a while in the wide corridors. He walked by different size horizontal shafts and niches, from very simple quarters with barely any additions beside a wooden bed to richly decorated ones with animal skins, horns, amulets, and dry flowers. The place looked like an underground city with only a small part kept as a salt mine.

The looks he encountered during his walk varied from curiosity to disbelief and fear.

"There you are," he heard Stamat saying while emerging from

one of the shafts he had just passed.

"Where have you been?" asked Goran.

"Well, I decided to take your advice and talked to as many of the regular dwarfs as I could. I got up very early and I am glad I did. Otherwise, I wouldn't have been able to catch them before breakfast. Because very soon, they all are going to have their communal breakfast in the big eating hall, as they call it. Come along, I will explain everything as we walk. It's worse than I thought."

"What do you mean by communal breakfast?"

"You see," said Stamat, "they found a way to get everyone involved in this establishment. Nobody is thinking of leaving. They have dwarfs that go out to hunt daily, dwarfs that cook for everyone, dwarfs that make things such as furniture for everyone, dwarfs, who extract salt so that they could barter with other dwarf communities in the area, and so on."

"How is this so bad?" asked Goran. "Nobody goes hungry and cold, and once we prove there is no danger to live outside anymore, they'll all move out."

"You would think so. The only problem is that the dwarfs I spoke with already knew that. They figured out that God Perun was no longer trying to kill them. But they feel so comfortable in this mine that they simply don't want to leave. They don't think living out in the open with fresh air and plenty of sunshine is worth abandoning their comfort. They don't feel like dealing with the challenges that outside world would inevitably bring. But it's even worse than that. Their leaders do their best to encourage them to stay."

"What are you saying?"

"I am saying their leaders want to keep the established order and they are constantly looking for reasons to convince the dwarfs to stay. I think the dwarfs are afraid to leave not because of God Perun but because of their leaders. By the way, do you know what the main requirement for a dwarf who wants to be a hunter is? They have to be either a leader or a direct descendant of one."

"This means most of them have hardly ever seen sunlight? They are held imprisoned, and they don't even realize it!"

"It looks like it, Goran!" said Stamat, his voice shaking.

"Hey, listen, maybe other dwarf settlements are not as well organized. Maybe dwarfs there are not that comfortable. We can try those."

"I don't know, Goran. I have been doing this all my life—as far as I can remember. I was very young when my mother died and my father and I left our mine for good. Until this morning, I had a great hope that I would finally accomplish what my father started all these years ago. Not anymore. Now, I just feel tired. I think I will—"

"Good morning, folks!" said a very cheerful female voice and interrupted the conversation. "My name is Draga."

"Good morning, Draga," said Goran half-heartedly

"So," continued Draga, "I understand you are here to purchase some salt. Which mine or cave did you come from again?"

"We didn't come from a mine or a cave," said Stamat dryly. "I have been living outside, in the open, most of my life, and my friend here, Goran, who is not a dwarf, has always lived in a hut. He is a human. But I think you know all about them now, don't you?"

Draga, who did not expect that kind of answer, was taken aback. She pursed her lips and gave Goran a long questioning look.

"Yes," she said at last, "It has come to our attention. Our wisest leaders have been observing the current situation. And they have concluded that as long as we don't leave our underground homes, we are not in danger."

"But," interrupted Goran, "God Perun is not interested in killing you anymore! You saw what happened to us. I used to be an ispolin. Although he was not happy with us, he did not kill us off— he simply changed us into humans! Isn't that enough proof?"

"Ah, but this is what he wants us to think! The reality is, he had found a subtler way to kill us. Once we decide the danger had passed and leave our underground dwellings, we will inevitably come across humans. And humans are far from what ispolins used to be. We have reasons to fear humans. They are almost as smart as we are. Humans will not want us around. They will finish us off. We know this is God Perun's plan for us!"

Goran could not believe his ears.

"Wait! What?" he screamed at Draga, "You are telling me that God Perun, in his infinite wisdom, took his time and energy to turn all ispolins into humans, so that the humans can destroy the dwarfs once they become aware of their existence, I don't know, years or even centuries from now, only to save himself some thunder and lightning that could have achieved the same result instantaneously?"

"The Divine works in mysterious ways," said Draga calmly.

"You are not making any sense! Bring us to your leaders!" screamed Goran.

"Goran, don't bother," said Stamat. "Draga, two kilos of salt, please, and then we'll be on our way."

***

Earlier that morning the snowfall turned into a blizzard. The mortar was flying high above snow-clad trees and meadows as its two passengers were trying to adjust its course and steady it up. The freezing gusts of wind were not making their efforts easier. Goran had no idea how Stamat still knew which way to go.

Besides the fly commands he was giving to Goran and the mortar, Stamat had not said a word. Goran tried to talk about the salt mine, Draga, and what they would do with all the salt they bought. He asked Stamat where they were going next and when they would get there. He tried to talk about anything. Stamat did not answer. He had a resigned look on his face Goran had never seen before.

That scared Goran. He would have much rather dealt with a very angry Stamat than a depressed one. He decided that it might be better to give Stamat some space. After all, unless the mortar crashed, Stamat knew where to find him.

After a few hours, the mortar started descending and then landed outside a small village. The blizzard had no intention of dying down. Goran looked around. He couldn't see more than a few feet around him. He jumped down and turned around to help Stamat down when the dwarf said, "Remember when I told you how my father and I broke into God Perun's palace last summer?"

"Yes?" said Goran suspiciously, not sure where this conversation was going.

"And I told you about the Book of History of Everything, and how I accidentally came across your story and that's how we knew where to find you."

"Yes!"

"Well, I never told you this, but I also read the very first page of the book. And you know what it said?"

"No..."

"I remember it word for word. It said, 'At the beginning, there was Nothing. And Nothing was everything. Nothing was everywhere. Nothing was all there was. And this lasted for a very long time. Then suddenly, Nothing gave birth to Light and everything changed. Many, many eons later, one gloomy afternoon, God Perun woke up and found himself on the top of a mountain, on a small planet in a very indistinguishable part of Everything. He had no idea how he ended up on the top of a mountain, and what had happened before he got there. He did not even know what he looked like, but knew who he was—God Perun, the supreme and unsurpassed god of thunder and lightning.'"

"Interesting," muttered Goran, who still had no clue why Stamat was telling him all this.

"I am tired, Goran. Very tired. I have been living like this for years. It has always been my father and I against our whole race. And now, it's just me. I don't want to do this anymore. I thought about it.

The salt mine doesn't look so bad. I am going back there. Maybe, eventually I will settle down. Maybe, I will find another purpose."

Goran did not know how to react. He was cold, hungry, and was getting very angry. But he knew that yelling at Stamat would do more harm than good.

"Stamat," said Goran quietly, barely able to control himself, "I get it. I see what's going on. All these years you have been trying to achieve something with no success. But there is no reason to quit now. Not until you have tried everything in your power. I know there are a few more locations we can visit. We picked a bad time, that's all. Let's take a break for the winter. Nobody wants to be outside in this weather anyway. We'll try again in the spring. I bet we'll have better luck then."

"Maybe Draga was right," said Stamat as if he did not hear Goran's argument. "Maybe they have it all figured out. Who am I to disrupt their well-organized lives?"

"I hope you are joking!"

"I am not, and I am sorry I have wasted your time. I have to go now."

"Did you get the same disease that Draga is suffering from? Is there anything in that salt mine that causes dwarfs' minds to stop functioning?" yelled Goran, now completely losing his self-control. "And why in the Underworld did you tell me about the first page of the Book of History of Everything? What does it have to do with all this?"

"Don't you see," yelled Stamat back, "if Nothing can give

birth to Light, then Light might turn back into Nothing, and everything would have been in vain, anyway. I should stop wasting my time trying to change things."

"And what if Light never turns into Nothing! You are missing the only chance you have to help your people. Maybe there are dwarfs out there that are waiting for someone like you to encourage them to take the first step!"

"You can be that someone, Goran. I am not going to stop you. But I am done. Og pu!" yelled Stamat, and with that, the mortar made a sudden movement upwards and quickly disappeared into the skies, leaving Goran behind.

Goran felt as if someone had just dumped a bucket of ice water on his head. A few minutes later he started walking aimlessly through the foot-deep snow. It was not until much later that he realized he was approaching his village. At least Stamat had been kind enough to give him a ride home.

***

Stamat had been flying for a couple of hours when he recognized the outline of the cave he was about to reach. He and his father did not frequent that particular cave. They were familiar with all the caves and mines in the area and knew better to stay away from that one.

This time, however, Stamat knew he had to go inside and face one of the most unpleasant creatures he had ever known—if he wanted to find the only one who could help him.

He entered the cave cautiously, his hand in his pocket firmly holding the golden apple. Although he knew he would find recovering in this cave a very weak shadow of a god, he also knew he could never underestimate the ruler of the Underworld. But he was not prepared for what he saw when he reached the main chamber. Lamya, the unpleasant creature he dreaded to see again, was sitting on the floor by a fireplace, stirring something in a big pot. A snake, missing a part of his lower body, was lying curled up on a big rock next to it, observing Lamya. Stamat sensed tension between the two. None of them noticed his entrance.

"My Lord," he heard Lamya saying, "are you not satisfied by the abundance of mice I have been providing? Have you not been enjoying the small rabbits and moles I bring in occasionally? Why do I have to cook the mice with all these other ingredients?"

"Lamya, Lamya, Lamya," said God Veles, visibly running out of patience, "as I already explained to you many of times, although I am still a snake, I do not enjoy raw meat any more. As I have regained some of my power, my taste for food has changed. Pretty soon, I will require bigger and tastier animals to eat—excluding birds, of course. You will soon be hunting for pigs, boars, and even cows. Now add some onions and spices, please, and keep stirring! One would think you hate cooking for me!"

"I don't even cook for myself," murmured Lamya.

Being in her serpentine form—a long snake with a woman's body from the waist up—she slid away from the pot to grab some onions stored by the wall a few feet away. Before she could reach them, however, she sniffed the air, looked around, and saw Stamat.

"We have a visitor, my Lord!" she said quietly. God Veles jumped and almost fell off the rock he was lying on. This made Lamya sneer discreetly with quiet satisfaction.

"Please allow me to kill him," she said after God Veles regained his control.

"Most certainly not—not before we find out why he is here. My bet is he got lost and wandered here by mistake. Dwarf, speak!"

"I am here to make you an offer—one, I think, you can't afford to refuse!" spoke Stamat firmly.

Lamya let out a dry, unpleasant laugh.

"Silence!" hissed the snake.

"I have something you need," said Stamat, and he pulled out the golden apple from his pocket.

God Veles flinched. He almost ordered Lamya to attack, but caught himself just in time after quickly realizing that the dwarf was not there to kill him. After he regained composure, he spoke. "Dwarf, remind me of your name again."

"Stamat, Veehar's son."

"That's right. How is your father doing these days? The last time I saw him, he was on the ground writhing in pain right after I had disowned him of his own golden apples. Where were you that day? We all missed you!" chuckled God Veles, but Stamat let this pass by his ears and did not react.

"And now," continued God Veles, "here you are, offering me one! Let me ask you something. Have you lost your mind?"

"Lamya is not my favorite type of dragon," said Stamat, "and

I desire nothing more than to get out of here as soon as possible. So, I'll be very direct. I don't need the golden apple, but I reckon you do. However, you can do something for me that nobody else can, and if you agree to do it, the golden apple is yours. And, by the way, you will not order Lamya to attack me now, because by the time she gets to this entrance I might be gone. Or I might not be—she might be able to catch me, but why risk losing the golden apple forever?"

"What do you want?" God Veles asked after thinking for a minute about what Stamat had said and admitting to himself that the dwarf was right.

"I want you to make it so that dwarfs abandon their underground homes forever and live out in the open again. I want everything to go back to the way it used to be, before God Perun tried to destroy us."

That was not what God Veles expected. It was not an easy request, even for a god, but he was not going to decline the offer.

"It will be done by the end of spring" said Veles. "It can't happen overnight."

"I understand," said Stamat. "I will be waiting for you at midnight after the last day of spring by the Old Salt Mine. If you have fulfilled your promise, the golden apple is yours. Farewell."

Just when Stamat was about the leave the cave, God Veles called after him.

Stamat stopped and turned around.

"Tell me," said God Veles, "why did you come to me? Isn't God Perun the safer choice? He needs the golden apple as much as I do."

"As much as I don't like the idea of dealing with a trickster," said Stamat quietly, "nothing can make me deal with my father's killer."

CHAPTER 9
DAY OF THE KUKERI

By the time Goran got home, the snowstorm had died out. Exhausted, he fell asleep and did not wake up until the following morning.

Weeks passed, and winter spread its frozen grip throughout the land, bringing frigid winds that swept tirelessly over the bare fields. The days grew shorter and the nights longer. Goran spent a lot of time sleeping. When he was not asleep, he was thinking. Stamat's decision did not make sense. Goran tried to remember everything that happened between the time they went to the Strawberry Cave and the moment Stamat left him in the outskirts of his village. Try as he might, Goran could not find any clues that would explain what made Stamat change his mind so suddenly.

When Goran ran out of provisions, he went to the only market in his village, hoping that it would still be open this late in the year. He was pleasantly surprised to see that someone had raised a wooden structure around it, which now sheltered dozens of tables loaded with grapes, apples, pears, potatoes, garlic, spices, and fresh and dried meat.

Goran also saw a few tables covered with fur coats and boots, pottery, soap, brandy, and wine. He deliberately walked around the tables slowly, observing his neighbors and stopping frequently to greet them. He knew most of them, but at the same time they were all strangers now, strangers he once knew very well, who turned out to be not how he remembered them at all.

By one of the tables, Goran saw his neighbor, Peter, who apparently had not forgotten the brandy brewing incident and was unhappy with this unexpected encounter.

When Goran had left his village earlier that fall, different and sometimes contradictory rumors quickly started to spread. Some said he moved away for good but left dark magic in his house so that nobody else could move in. Others thought he had found a treasure and moved to a faraway land so that he could spend it without raising questions. Yet, there were those who believed that Goran had sold his soul to Vodnik—or worse, to God Veles—in exchange for a big sum of money, something in the range of one hundred perperos. As for Peter, he was convinced that Goran had simply lost his mind and wandered off into the nearby woods.

Peter looked around quickly hoping that an escape plan would conveniently present itself, but there were no other shoppers nearby at that moment, and Goran was standing on the only path out of the area. Peter cursed his luck in his head and braced himself.

"Goran, hi!" Peter forced himself to say.

"Hi Peter!" replied Goran just as awkwardly.

"Listen, Peter," continued Goran, regaining some of his confidence, "I think I owe you an apology. I know I have said some things in the past that have made you feel uncomfortable and have probably made you question my sanity."

"Ummm," Peter hesitated.

"I was only joking then," said Goran.

"Ummm, okay, no problem," said Peter hastily, concentrating his attention on a goat's head displayed on one of the tables a couple of feet from him.

Goran did not see the goat's head until he followed Peter's eyes. Then, he realized he was in the middle of a section of the market dedicated to the Day of the Kukeri.

Goran had completely forgotten about the Day of the Kukeri.

Every year on the ninth day after the winter solstice, all men in Goran's village put on elaborate, scary-looking fur costumes and walked and danced through the streets to scare away evil spirits. Goran had admired the ingenuity and imagination some of his neighbors, even when they were ispolins, had put into crafting the most intricate costumes, the most grotesque masks, and the biggest and loudest copper bells.

The bells were usually attached to the belt of the costume, and their only purpose was to be as loud as possible, so that any evil spirit lurking nearby would be permanently deafened and scared away.

The oversized padded costumes were usually made from the pelts of sheep and goats, but the crafting of the masks were how the village men fully expressed their creativity. Some masks were made of wood, some were made of fur and feathers, but the one thing they all had in common was the disturbing and horrifying facial features they tried to achieve, mainly by using goat horns, bones, plenty of dye, colorful threads, beads, and ribbons.

And then, there were those who would attach a goat's head to the front of an already terrifying mask.

The kukeri walked and danced through the streets from dusk until dawn to make sure all evil spirits in the area were scared away and would not return to the village. At least not until the next Day of the Kukeri.

Evil spirits were doomed, but God Veles did not mind the festivities. He would sometimes done a costume and mask, and walk around with the rest of the kukeri.

Not this year, though. For the time being, he was stuck in Lamya's cave, and Stamat knew this. There was no better time for him to mingle with the local humans, in his heavy coat and oversized winter hat that covered most of his head and face. With so many humans of all ages walking around the market, who would suspect that he was not a human child, but a dwarf, one of the few thousand left in the world, whose race would probably be extinct in a couple of centuries?

Stamat was curious. Except for Goran, he had not met any humans. They were supposed to be better, he remembered Goran saying, better than both ispolins and dwarfs, even better than samodivas. Stamat highly doubted the last statement. Nobody, not even dwarfs, was better than samodivas. He could not imagine a more sophisticated creature, possessing all the old knowledge that dwarfs had mastered, but surpassing them in physical strength, healing powers, and application of magic—not to mention physical perfection.

No wonder God Perun had sacrificed Zara when he created humans. Stamat thought of Zara, and the realization that he would never see her again suddenly struck him. And there, in that foreign place, surrounded by creatures who were oblivious of how it all came to be, but who, nevertheless, would inherit his great race, he let his tears flow freely, not aware of the curious looks he had started to attract. He turned around to head to the exit but bumped into Peter, who had just finished talking to Goran and was making his way out.

"Are you lost, kid?" asked Peter.

"No," replied Stamat, "But if you need to know, a dear friend of mine was killed because of you!"

Peter instantly regretted asking the question.

"What are you talking about?" he asked, further disturbed by the kid's deep voice and strange facial features.

Stamat looked at Peter and repeated slowly, "My friend, Zara, a samodiva, was killed because of you!"

"What is a samodiva?" asked Peter. The fairly good mood he was in as a result of the reassuring conversation he had just had with Goran was disappearing faster than a snowflake on Stamat's tear-soaked scarf.

"Samodiva is the most ethereal and perfect creature you would ever meet. But you could only meet them in the deepest parts of the forest, if you are lucky enough, or unlucky, depending on the circumstances!"

With that, Stamat left Peter very confused and wondering why he was always the one attracting the biggest lunatics in the area.

Stamat saw Goran standing by one of the tables covered with kukeri masks, costumes, and decorations. He must have decided to participate in the festivities this year. He was so involved in an animated conversation with the seller that Stamat decided he would not find a better time to stop by Goran's hut.

He hurried back outside and made his way through the narrow path leading to Goran's hut. He pushed the door open and went straight to the pantry. As he expected, the shelves stood almost empty, but Stamat knew that later that day they would be stacked and overflowing with provisions. The small gap between the bottom shelf and the floor was all he needed.

He left the hut and headed outside the village, where his mortar was waiting for him. In a few hours he arrived at the summit of the Mountain of Perun and made his way through the deep snow toward the underground dwelling he and Veehar built a long time ago. They had survived a few winters there, and this time it was not going to be different.

***

"So, did you find him?" God Veles asked Lamya, who had just returned to her cave and assumed her serpentine form.

"No, my love," she replied, "by the time I got outside, he was gone."

"Of course. He is not stupid. You should have checked the nearby woods first. I bet he was hiding mere feet away from the cave, waiting for you to fly by before he could make a clean exit."

"My Lord, you know that once I turn into a dragon, I can only follow the orders I was given prior to the transformation, and you didn't tell me to check the woods first."

God Veles knew she was right, but needed to take his anger out on someone. He was about to say something to start a bigger fight, but changed his mind. It was not worth it. He still needed Lamya. He just had to be patient. He had estimated that in a couple of months, his tail would grow enough so that he would completely recover and transform back into his divine form—the god of the Underworld.

However, he still had no idea how to find God Perun, and more importantly, how to get rid of him once and for all. Thanks to Stamat, he might be able to get his hands on a golden apple, but that would not be enough.

Although God Veles spent most of his time thinking of his revenge, he could not come up with a viable plan. To add to the frustration, he had the feeling he was forgetting something but did not know what.

Despite the harsh conditions outside the cave, Lamya went hunting almost daily. And since humans could not see the she-dragon, Lamya did not have to hide or wait for the nightfall. She would often snatch a goat or a sheep from the nearby villages. Almost always, native predators were blamed for these crimes. The locals spent long hours setting up traps and hunting for wolves, foxes and minks, with no noticeable results.

Although Lamya was still taking care of God Veles's meals, she was growing more and more distant. His constant teasing and criticism, even if out of boredom and frustration, were getting worse. In order not to bite his head off in his sleep, she had to constantly remind herself of the prize that was awaiting her. "One day," she remembered God Veles saying, "you will rule this world by my side!"

One day, Lamya the she-dragon would become Lamya the goddess.

***

On the ninth day after the winter solstice, God Veles was abruptly awakened by a strong vibration in his jaw. He realized this was caused by the ringing of hundreds of cowbells and suddenly remembered it was the Day of the Kukeri. How could he have forgotten! It was his favorite ispolin holiday. Back in the day, he would put on a kukeri costume and, covered from head to toe, mingle and celebrate with the ispolins in the village.

"Lamya!" he shouted, causing the she-dragon to drop the pig she was disemboweling, "get me to the village! It's the Day of the Kukeri!"

"Right away, my Lord," said Lamya, who was always glad to take a break from cooking.

"Wait!" cried God Veles. "When we get to the village, you fly over the crowd and drop me on top of someone's head. It doesn't matter who. As long as they wear a big furry hat, and most of them will, they won't know I am there. Bring me back once the festival is over, unless I call for you earlier."

The snake coiled around Lamya's wrist as she was exiting the cave. Once they got outside, she quickly transformed into a three-headed green she-dragon and took off.

As instructed, after a short flight Lamya descended over the crowd, which had already assembled in the big open space in the center of the village. The air was offensively cold, but this did not deter hundreds of kukeri from dancing, walking around, and making tremendous noise. As always, nobody saw Lamya. She gently placed the god of the Underworld on top of the largest and furriest hat she could see and retreated to the closest roof, misplacing a few roof tiles in the process.

God Veles was not the only one whose curiosity led him to the village on the Day of the Kukeri. Since his first encounter with a human, Vodnik had been waiting impatiently for this day. Now, under his heavy costume and huge mask, he could finally take a good look at the new creatures everyone in the forest was talking about. Smaller than ispolins but much quicker, they said. "Nonetheless," he thought, "they can't be faster than me."

It just so happened that Lamya had dropped God Veles on the top of Vodnik's huge fur mask. Vodnik did not feel anything, and neither was he able to smell the snake. His extensive fishy odor, however, hit God Veles's olfactory system right away. God Veles cursed his luck. Of all the participants he could have landed on, it had to be the Great Vodnik of the Eastern Marshlands!

He had always despised Vodnik. A slimy, obnoxious scoundrel who was too lazy to tidy up his own home and, instead, enslaved the souls of the ispolins he had drowned. And those were the lucky ones! Most of the captured souls spend the eternity shut in small glass jars. Those souls belonged to the god of the Underworld! Veles never made a big deal out of this before, but once he recovered, things would change! A lot would change! He just had to be patient.

Vodnik's fishy body odor had started to attract attention. Veles noticed that, but he knew he had nothing to worry about. He had curled up deeply in the thick fur hat, which was keeping him warm and well hidden. Suddenly, he felt someone's presence. Someone driven by curiosity had come too close to Vodnik. The snake carefully lifted his head up, trying not to reveal his presence. The stranger was wearing a mask in the form of a rooster's head. The eyes were elongated, and the beak was long and crooked, which gave the rooster an angry appearance.

God Veles's reaction came before his brain could tell him it was only a mask and there was nothing to worry about. His scream made Vodnik fall backward, hit his head on the ground, and lose his mask. It also woke up Lamya, who was taking a nap on the roof, completely undisturbed by the loud noises around her. She flew down to the ground, scooped up the mortified God Veles, and flew back up over the village and the forest as fast as she could.

As always, nobody saw Lamya, but a dozen people saw and recognized Vodnik. People quickly forgot they were in the middle of scaring away evil spirits and ran off in panic. Vodnik ran off, too. He did not want to attract more attention.

Goran, who happened to wander close by, saw everything but did not run. He recognized Vodnik and wondered what he was doing in the village. Peter ran past Goran and for a few seconds their eyes met. Goran quickly looked away, but Peter had already stopped. He stared at Goran. At that moment he knew that somehow this whole situation could be traced back to Goran, just like all the other strange and inexplicable events he was unfortunate to witness in the past few months.

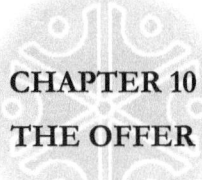

CHAPTER 10

THE OFFER

Curled tightly around Lamya'a claw, God Veles was trying to pull himself together. Just when he thought he had calmed down enough to venture a look around, Lamya flew by a flock of ravens resting on a big walnut tree. The birds noticed. They sized up the green she-dragon with great curiosity. After a short consideration, however, they decided it was not worth the risk.

This encounter was about to cause the god of the Underworld a new wave of anxiety, when suddenly he remembered how much he hated ravens. He hated them more than he hated any other living creature on the planet, except for God Perun, of course. Intelligent, fearless, and spiteful, they had never showed any veneration of him, not even the slightest respect for his divine essence. On the other hand, they did not care much about God Perun, either. It was time for them to learn a lesson. If only he were ready...

No. He was not going to wait any longer. He might be injured, but he was still a god! And not just any god! He let go of Lamya and fell down toward the icy river underneath. Several ravens saw that and flew after him. They thought he was a normal snake.

Croaking fiercely, they were getting closer and closer. He glared at them. There was no hesitation, no fear, not even hatred. Their life belonged to him. They were at his mercy now, as they had always been. One of the ravens caught his eye and horror swept over it. It recognized who the snake was and how angry the god was at them. It screeched to warn the others and tried to change the direction of its flight, but it was too late.

God Veles was as surprised as the ravens were. His desire to kill them had transformed his snake body into an Imperial Eagle—majestic and powerful. His talons had already snatched the body of the raven who had had the misfortune to get too close. The eagle's powerful beak pierced the raven's head.

The birds had gathered too much momentum to be able to veer off of their initial course of flight. God Veles let go of the dead raven and attacked another one. Within moments a few more lost their lives.

Lamya cried out cautiously and started circling over what was forming to be a formidable carnage. Finally, more and more ravens were able to scatter and escape. The screeching subsided.

Still surprised but extremely happy with what had just happened, a very confident Imperial Eagle was making his way toward a dry and cozy cave, closely followed by the cave's very confused owner.

Lamya did not know what to think. She was not sure if she could trust a lover who chose so unexpectedly to transform into her archenemy.

The Imperial Eagle, God Perun's favorite bird, was the only creature who was known to be able to defeat Lamya. She had no idea why God Veles chose to turn himself into that particular bird. His new form made her nervous and a little offended.

"I thought you had fear of birds!" said Lamya after assuming her half-snake, half-woman form.

"I used to, my dear, and maybe I still do," said God Veles, hopping around with excitement, "but don't you see what had just happened? I am not stuck in my serpentine form any longer! I am free! I can finally start implementing my plan!"

Lamya had never seen him so excited.

"My Lord, I hope you still plan to destroy God Perun!"

"Of course, Lamya! This world will be mine! The Underworld apparently is doing just fine without me, although I think I have found the perfect ruler for it!"

"Don't you mean 'ours'—this world will be ours?"

"Don't worry, my dear! I know what I have promised to you. You will rule this world by my side!"

"How did you do it, my Lord? How were you able to turn into an Imperial Eagle?"

"It's a mystery even to me, Lamya. The ravens were about to tear me in pieces, when it suddenly happened. Because I am a god, I can't be killed by a bunch of ravens. I guess this transformation needed to happen, otherwise the natural order would have been violated."

"When do you think you'll transform into your divine form?"

"Soon, Lamya, I am sure it will happen soon."

***

God Veles spent the next few days flying around and enjoying his newly-found freedom. He knew where Stamat lived and paid him a visit. He waited for the dwarf to leave his underground den and went inside to look for the golden apple. As he expected, the golden apple was not there.

He felt comfortable in his new body. Nobody dared to bother him. He started to wonder if he could even get close to God Perun without being recognized.

He knew that only God Perun and his trusted Imperial Eagles could get inside the Tree of Life, God Perun's palace. It was worth trying. He was done waiting. The longer he waited, the better the chances were that God Perun would get hold of the golden apple himself.

The Tree of Life stood invisible on the top of the Mountain of Perun. It became visible only during a total solar eclipse, which happened once every five hundred years. But even then, one would not be able to see its top. According to the legends, its crown reached the havens and its roots spread deep into the earth and touched the realm of the Underworld.

It was during the last total solar eclipse when Stamat and his father succeeded in sneaking into the Tree of Life and stealing three golden apples from God Perun's collection. God Veles was impressed. Although he had, unknowingly to them, provided a little help, the dwarfs did most of the work themselves.

God Veles did not expect to find any golden apples left in the Tree of Life. Now, in his Imperial Eagle form, he flew right in.

***

Inside the palace, God Perun was sitting by the big wooden round table. He had long abandoned reading through the Book of History of Everything. He had abandoned his ocean palace and his hobby. He was staring at a spot on the wall by the spiral stairwell—a hollow spot where he used to store one of his golden apples. He looked at the Imperial Eagle who had just appeared and stretched his arm.

The bird hesitated but landed on God Perun's arm. He sensed something was amiss. God Perun, so fond of Imperial Eagles, did not pet him.

"Do you know where the golden apple is? I need to find a golden apple. Can you look for it?" said God Perun in a dry voice.

"Where do you want me to look, master?" asked the bird.

"One of the golden apples was taken by the winds. It could be anywhere. But the one that was lost in the battle is still somewhere on the top of the mountain, unless someone has already found it."

"I will look for it, master!" said the bird and flew away, as it did not want to push its luck much further.

"Another golden apple," thought God Veles as he was flying away from the palace with a speed hardly ever achieved by a normal Imperial Eagle. "So there are two golden apples left, and only I know who has one of them."

Soon he reached a long, partially-frozen river, the residence of the Great Vodnik of the Eastern Marshlands. He thought how useful it would be if he could temporarily turn himself back into a snake. This time, it took only a thought, and God Veles found himself plunging into the icy water below in a form of a water snake.

The river was deeper than he expected. He was still missing a small part of his tail, but that did not hinder his swimming. He knew the Chamber of the Locked Souls was nearby. That was where Vodnik kept his collection of glass jars. Each jar contained a soul of a victim he had drowned. He used to keep his victims' bodies as slaves but soon found out that he wasted more time explaining a task than it should take his slaves to complete it, and got rid of them. But he kept the souls, as the number of souls locked in the jars was directly proportional to his social status and reputation.

What God Veles did not expect to see in the Chamber of the Locked Souls was Vodnik's daughter, Morna.

Morna was a creature who often provoked confusion and mixed feelings. Even in the old days, when the ispolins ruled the land and magical creatures were easier to find, Morna was somewhat of an outcast. She was the daughter of Kikimora and Vodnik, undoubtedly two very foul creatures, but those who got to know her better soon discovered that she did not have much in common with either of them.

At first glance she looked like her mother—the same slender physique, long brown hair, and pale skin. But her facial features were very soft, and the small bump on her nose made her otherwise bland face look more intriguing.

It was even harder to believe she was Vodnik's daughter—until one saw her swim. She could stay underwater without resurfacing for hours and hours on end.

God Veles was quite surprised to see her in the Chamber of the Locked Souls, mainly because he had forgotten, like so many, about her existence. Otherwise, he would have remembered that the chamber was where she spent most of her time. Morna loved looking at the jars and cleaning the thin film of algae which formed on their surfaces. Sometimes, she would watch a soul bumping into the sides of the jar in a futile attempt to break free, and would try to calm it down by gently stroking the jar. Often the soul would slow down and follow her fingers.

For reasons no one could ever figure out, Morna also adored her father. They spent countless hours sitting on logs, playing cards and talking. When she sensed that Vodnik was in a particularly good mood, she would try to convince him to let the trapped souls go. He would become quiet for a few minutes and say, "I know you think I am cruel to keep them in jars, but you are too young to understand now. I need them."

"But why?" she would say. "You have me, father!"

He would sigh and not answer.

***

Morna must have sensed someone else was in the chamber because she suddenly turned around. A snake was watching her, curled up by one of the big boulders lying on the river floor. It started swimming toward her. Morna saw the snake and almost drop the jar she was cleaning.

"Don't be afraid," said the snake, "I am God Veles. I won't hurt you."

Morna did not know how she heard and understood what the snake was saying, but she clearly heard God Veles's voice in her head.

She carefully placed the jar she was holding back on the shelf. She pointed at her mouth, trying to explain that she could not talk under water.

"I know you can't, Morna. But if you look me in the eyes while talking to me in your head, I will be able to hear you," said God Veles.

"Are you looking for my father?" asked Morna, somehow not sufficiently impressed by the fact that the god of the Underworld had just showed up in her father's river.

"I was actually looking for the trapped souls," said Veles. "You see, all these souls belong to me, and Vodnik has no right to keep them."

"You came here to free them up and send them to the Underworld?"

"That is my plan, eventually," said Veles smiling. "I know you are very fond of them and have taken good care of them, for which I am very grateful!"

Morna did not know what to say. This was all she had ever wanted, but now that her wish was about to come true, she was not sure she was ready to let the souls go.

She did not have to come up with an answer after all. At that moment the Great Vodnik of the Eastern Marshlands dove into the Chamber of the Locked Souls and almost hit the large boulder God Veles was swimming next to. Morna jumped back, startled. She caught Vodnik's eyes and pointed toward the snake. Without hesitation, Vidnik grabbed the snake and swam to the surface.

Morna followed her father up quickly and reached the surface just in time to see Vodnik smashing the snake against a big stone lying on the side of the riverbank.

"What are you doing?" yelled Morna, "this is not an ordinary snake. This is the god of the Underworld!"

As if to confirm Morna's words, God Veles immediately turned into a very angry Imperial Eagle.

"Vodnik!" bellowed Veles.

"I am truly sorry, my Lord!" said Vodnik in a trembling voice. "I was only protecting my daughter. I thought she was in danger! Please forgive me!"

"You are lucky today, Vodnik! Very lucky!" cried Veles, overwhelmed with anger from the painful encounter with the rock but at the same time filled with great joy from the fact he was able to turn back into an Imperial Eagle at will.

"I have an offer for you that you won't be able to refuse," chuckled the Imperial Eagle. "No, really, you will have no choice but accept it!"

Vodnik's heart sank. He had a very bad feeling about it.

"I want all your soul jars, along with the souls that are residing in them! They belong to me!"

"My Lord, please," cried Vodnik and fell on his knees, "they are my treasure. Please don't take them from me. Without them I am nothing. I will be the laughingstock of all my cousins up north."

"Not when they hear what you got for them!"

"What do you mean, my Lord?"

"I appoint you a ruler of the Underworld! I am pretty busy these days and I need someone to keep an eye on it. And because I am in a great mood today, I allow you to take your daughter with you."

"My Lord! I don't know what to say." Vodnik was quite shocked. Still on his knees, he started kissing the eagle's talons.

Suddenly, Vodnik paused, turned quite pale, which was easily noticeable with his green complexion, and said, "My Lord, do Morna and I have to die first in order to get to the Underworld?"

"A good question, Vodnik, a very good question! Normally yes, but this time I will make an exception for you two. After all, Morna was such a good keeper of the jarred souls. Let it be known that I am a fair god, not the trickster everyone thinks I am." Veles winked at Morna.

An hour later, Veles was flying back to the Tree of Life followed by a swarm of souls still in their jars, as if an attractive force was keeping them locked in an invisible field around the god of the Underworld.

Morna, still not sure how to feel about the recent events, turned to her father and said, "Father, do you know how to get to the Underworld without getting us killed?"

"I know a way, Morna, if memory serves me right..." said Vodnik, still pretty shocked himself.

God Veles reached the Tree of Life and flew right in. He knew he was not ready for a battle with God Perun, but he had to take the risk. He had to leave the jars there. They had to stay in the palace hidden, awaiting his command when the time would finally come.

The Imperial Eagle looked around frantically, ready to dash out of the palace at the first sight of God Perun. But the god of thunder was not there. God Veles could not believe his luck. He was alone in the Tree of Life.

He started flying higher and higher along the walls. As if following a command, one by one the jars separated from the group and landed on the empty spots which once housed the golden apples until the day God Perun summoned them away and melted them off.

After the last jar found its spot, the Imperial Eagle flew back down and landed on the big wooden chair placed by the wall. He looked around. Still no sign of God Perun. The chair did not look like much. God Perun could have done better. One day, when all this belonged to God Veles, he would make sure to get himself a proper throne.

He glanced at the wooden table in the middle of the hall where the Book of History of Everything should be. It was not there. He would make sure it would be displayed on the table at all times. It tended to bring character to the place.

And the big tunnel in the middle of the floor that led to the

Underworld and opened on command would be sealed forever. He did not have to bother with the Underworld anymore. He would be the supreme god of this one.

Sunk deeply in his thoughts, God Veles did not notice the giant praying mantis creeping down the wall behind him. As it was moving quietly toward the clueless Imperial Eagle, its triangular head turned left and right to make sure there were no other intruders that needed to be taken care of. Its two compound eyes, made of thousands of miniature ones, were focusing on the eagle's torso. Now at a striking distance, it unleashed its powerful front legs and grabbed the eagle. The spikes beneath its front limbs pierced the eagle's flesh and pinned it.

The only thing that saved the Imperial Eagle was the fact that he was not an ordinary eagle. The praying mantis sensed that and hesitated for a second, which was just enough for God Veles to realize what was going on and to start pecking its eyes frantically. The praying mantis loosened its grip, and God Veles managed to slip away from its spikes. He dashed out of the hall and through the walls of the Tree of Life, blood dripping from his body.

As he realized with great relief that he was not gravely damaged, he was wondering why Perun was always so keen on using unconventional guards to watch over his property—a praying mantis for his palace, Dragon Zmei for his golden apple tree. Nonetheless, nothing would help the god of thunder the next time God Veles returned to the Tree of Life.

CHAPTER 11

THE DREAM

That winter—for the first time since he could remember, and to his great surprise—Goran was quite pleased with his life. Although it snowed a lot after the Day of the Kukeri, the temperatures stayed mild. Goran spent most of the days outside gathering wood. Soon, he realized he had more than he needed and started giving it away to his neighbors.

One day, out of boredom he carved a spoon from one of the logs lying around. It hardly looked like a spoon, but he enjoyed the process. It was not long before he tried carving a bowl. The more time he spent on it, the more he liked it. Then he carved another, and then another. His last two bowls looked so well made that he proudly gave them away. Word got around that whatever was wrong with Goran was gone, and he was now a normal member of the village. Even his neighbor Peter forgot all about his suspicions.

Nonetheless, there was one thing that was still bothering Goran. Sometimes late at night, lying on his wooden bed covered with bear skin, he pondered over the fate of the dwarfs. He could still not make sense of Stamat's decision. He could not believe Stamat gave up on his and his father's dream, after everything the two had accomplished and after everything Goran and Stamat went through this past fall.

He was contemplating going back to the Old Salt Mine in the spring and talking to the dwarfs again. But he knew it would be in vain. The dwarfs did not want to listen to one of their own; what were the chances they would listen to Goran! And besides, if Stamat did not care anymore, why should he?

Unlike Goran, God Veles did not feel that his life was improving much in the past few weeks. In fact, it had not moved in the right direction since he last transformed into an eagle and smuggled a bunch of souls locked in glass jars into God Perun's palace, the Tree of Life.

Try as he might, he could not get into his divine form. He tried a few tricks, which mainly involved putting himself in life-threatening situations, but he kept turning into different animals, according to the need of the moment. Consequently, the Imperial Eagle who plunged into the icy water of the God's Eye lake on the top of the Mountain of Perun turned immediately into a huge sturgeon, and then when the sturgeon reached the shore and jumped out of the water, it turned into a red fox, perfectly equipped to survive the harsh winter in the mountain.

God Veles started to get the disturbing suspicion that he was turning more and more into a true animal god.

As a desperate attempt to snap out of his animalistic nature, one gloomy winter morning he started a huge fight with Lamya, secretly hoping she would finally snap and try to kill him. Instead she looked at him in such a way that he truly wished he had never got himself involved with her in the first place. She then turned into a three-headed green she-dragon, took off, and never returned.

***

Goran was standing on the sea shore. The sea was calm. Small waves splashed cheerfully against the coarse sand and cooled off Goran's feet. It was a warm day. A step forward, and the water covered his knees. Another step, and the water was up to his waist. He turned around. The sea shore had disappeared and he was surrounded by water.

For the past few weeks Goran had had that same dream over and over. He did not mind it. The dream would always end there. But that night, it was different. Goran turned around. He was surrounded by water. He took a few steps forward. The water did not get any deeper, but the water surface was not as flat anymore.

As the sea was getting more and more agitated, the waves reached up to his shoulders, then over his head. He could no longer feel the bottom of the sea and started treading water in panic. He did not know which way to go, but this concern did not last long because he was distracted by a movement a few feet away from him. He thought he saw the end of an oversized snake tale. He dove in only to bump into a beautiful woman with long black hair and serpentine body.

Moments later Lamya was holding his head under the water. The last thought that struck his mind as he was drowning was that he would not suffer long—in a couple of minutes it would all be over.

Just before he was about to pass out, he felt Lamya's grip loosen. He opened his eyes and saw Veehar clinching onto Lamya's neck with all his strength, choking her. As Goran was swimming frantically toward the surface, he was wondering how Veehar knew Goran was in trouble and how he managed to show up just in time and save him, especially considering Veehar was supposed to be dead.

Goran woke up drenched in sweat with no question in his mind what he would be doing that day. Somehow, while he was getting used to his new life, he forgot that Veehar and Stamat saved his life that past summer when Goran, Spas, and Zara were on their quest to find the golden apple tree. He owed Veehar one last attempt to help the dwarfs, even if Stamat was not interested.

That very same day Goran left his home in a hurry. Since it was early spring and food was scarce, he took a small sack of provisions and tied it to a stick half his size. Then he flung the stick with the sack over his shoulder and headed to the Old Salt Mine.

After a week of walking, Goran had covered half of the distance to the mine. The mild weather continued its reign and Goran started to see more and more areas clear of snow and ice. On a few occasions he noticed the tiny stems of snowdrops breaking through the ground. "The first flower of spring," he thought, smiling. He always wondered how this small and delicate flower was able to find its way through the snow and withstand even the coldest weather.

"I knew you wouldn't be able to stay away from these woods

for long," said a voice that made him drop the sack.

It took him a couple of seconds to realize that the voice, which sounded familiar, came from above. Stamat, standing in Baba Yaga's mortar, was grinning at him.

"What are you doing here?" yelled Goran, partly happy to see Stamat, partly mad at him for startling him.

"Well, I thought about what you said and decided to give it one more try. But most of all, I started to get bored. Hop in!" said Stamat, lowering the mortar almost to the ground.

"We will be there in no time!" said Stamat, seemingly excited as he was directing the mortar to ascend.

"Do you have a plan?" asked Goran.

"Yes," responded Stamat, "I always have a plan. But I will fill you in the details when we get there. Basically, we will want to show my distrusting brothers and sisters the beauty of nature, especially this time of the year. I think that once they see what spring, and I mean real spring, looks like outside the cave, they will cave in." Stamat laughed at his own joke.

"That's it? That's your plan?" Goran could not believe his ears.

"Trust me! We know most of them haven't seen much of the world outside the cave. So when they go outside and look at the hills around them, the river that flows nearby, the sky above them, they will feel as if the hand of God has created all these especially for them. Every single little flower, every tree, every bird, every late snowflake, everything. And they will feel very important. Something they have never felt before."

"Okay," agreed Goran, "and how do you know this is going to happen?"

"You'll see. For now, we have to think about how to convince as many of them as possible to go outside, even for a minute."

Stamat's plan, though worth considering, immediately set alarm bells ringing, bells which Goran could not ignore. The one word that was hanging like a black cloud in Goran's head and could not find a rational link to the rest of the plan was "god." Goran knew from experience that when dwarfs and gods mixed together, things quickly got out of hand.

"Stamat," said Goran cautiously, "when you said 'the hand of God', which god were you referring to exactly?"

But before Stamat could answer, he had to make a sharp turn to avoid colliding with an enormous Imperial Eagle.

The bird had appeared out of nowhere and was viciously attacking Stamat. Goran grabbed the pestle and tried to hit the bird with it, but it was as if the bird did not even notice.

"Why is this bird so mad at you?" cried Goran.

Stamat had no doubt who the bird was. He knew God Veles would get to the golden apple within seconds, one way or another, and both he and Goran would be killed. Without hesitating any longer, he pulled the golden apple out of his pocket and threw it at the bird.

At that moment, the bird was a few feet away. God Veles, or

any other god even slightly familiar with the way golden apples worked, would not be too worried. There was not nearly enough distance between Stamat and God Veles for a golden apple to cause any real damage. God Veles could have just let the golden apple hit him and fall on the ground. It would still be a perfectly functioning golden apple and the god would still be a perfectly healthy Imperial Eagle. A god could only be destroyed if hit by a golden apple cast by another god and at a proper distance.

God Veles, however, did not expect Stamat to cast the golden apple and risk destruction of everything around him. He reacted instinctively, and in his mind a golden apple flying at him meant death. Death, if you are an Imperial Eagle, but not anything to worry about if you are a god in your true divine form and hit by a golden apple thrown by a mortal.

God Veles reached out and grabbed the golden apple. It was then when he felt the transformation. Whatever was holding his divine essence entombed broke free. He had to become a true god again to avoid being killed. It was not a conscious choice. It was the nature of his existence, a universal law as real as the law that caused a golden apple to fall to the ground. He had finally returned to who he was meant to be—God Veles, the most versatile god, the most omnipotent god, the god of the Underworld, the god of wild beasts and domestic cattle, the god of trickery and magic.

And he was holding a golden apple in his hand!

Goran and Stamat, stunned by what they had just witnessed, were hovering helplessly in the mortar a few feet from the ground.

God Veles turned to Stamat and bellowed, "You really thought you could make a deal with me? You thought you and I were equal only because I was a snake! I will spare your life because you are an enemy of my enemy and because I have a soft spot for you—I would've been exactly like you if I were a mortal. And I would spare your friend's pitiful life only because today is the second best day of my life, and I am in a great mood! The best day of my life would be the day I finally destroy God Perun!"

God Veles turned back into an Imperial Eagle and took off, his triumphant laughter still echoing through the silent forest.

Stamat lowered the mortar and said to Goran, "Get out. I am going home."

"Oh, yes, I almost forgot you had one of these apples!" said Goran quietly.

"Actually, not all this time. You had it for a while too."

"What?"

"Well, you wouldn't expect me to hold on to it after I made a deal with God Veles, would you! I snuck into your hut one day and placed the apple under the bottom shelf of your food pantry. Nobody would look for it there!"

Goran had no idea what to say in response to that. After a few incoherent noises, he decided to change the subject.

"So, just like that, you are giving up again! Only because at some point things don't go according to your plan! And who in their right mind would make a deal with God Veles anyway!"

"I thought and still think he was my only hope. You saw how

stubborn dwarfs were. It doesn't matter now. I have failed. My father has failed. And I am glad he is not here to witness this."

"As you wish," said Goran calmly, screaming at Stamat in his head. "I'll carry on. I owe this to your father. He saved my life last summer. It's as simple as that."

Goran left Stamat standing by the mortar. He tried not to think of the latest turn of events and instead concentrated on making a faster pace. He did not know how long the mild weather would last.

CHAPTER 12
THE SNOWDROP FOREST

It was almost midnight when Goran got to the Old Salt Mine. The guard on duty recognized him from his last visit, and after Goran reassured him he was there to buy more salt and would pay in golden perperos, the guard let him in and showed him to an empty horizontal shaft where he could spend the rest of the night.

Goran found a couple of bear skins bundled neatly by the entrance. As he was spreading them down on the rocky floor to make himself a somewhat comfortable bed, he was wondering where the dwarfs had got them from and how much they had paid for them. It did not seem likely that they hunted the bears themselves, but Goran had learned to never underestimate dwarfs' ingenuity. Before he could ponder this more, he drifted off.

The following morning, Goran woke up to the sound of a bell. It was time for the communal breakfast. Goran waited a few minutes for the dwarfs to gather in the big breakfast hall. Standing by the entrance, he could see that the tables had already been set. A few dwarfs were walking around holding big trays with butter and jam sandwiches. Every dwarf was served two. There was one big teapot on every table.

The biggest table in the middle of the hall was occupied by several dwarfs, of whom Goran only recognized Draga. In a few minutes, after almost all the seats were taken and the sandwiches served, Draga stood up and gestured at the others to keep silence.

"Good morning, fellow residents of our safe and wonderful Old Salt Mine. Before we proceed with our breakfast, I want to talk to you about something that has come to our attention recently." She paused to make sure everyone was listening.

"It has come to our attention," continued Draga, "that the number of our customers has significantly increased in the past few months, and the increase is mainly due to humans, who now want to trade with us."

A collective gasp filled the breakfast hall. Draga looked very content at the effect her words had on her fellow residents. She waited a few seconds before raising her hand to stop the whispering that followed.

"Now," she continued, "although this might seem like alarming news, we shouldn't worry too much. We should be cautious, yes, but at the same time we should start planning for more salt production. We are forming a committee which will deal exclusively with this issue. Who wants to volunteer?"

A hesitant hand raised in the air.

"Yes! We have a volunteer?" asked Draga enthusiastically.

"N-no," stammered a very nervous looking dwarf, "I have a question. You've been telling us how dangerous humans are, and how they will wipe us out eventually. I wonder if it's wise of us to continue selling our salt to them because, you know, they might kill us."

A few dwarfs sitting around him nodded in agreement. Draga did not expect that. She cleared her throat and said, "Well, as I just said, we have to exercise caution, but I and the other leaders don't see why we shouldn't take advantage of the situation at least in the short run. Now, if there aren't any more questions, I will choose a few of you who I think would be great fits for the new committee!"

"Aren't the leaders the ones most suitable to form this committee?" asked another dwarf, but regretted it almost immediately.

"We, the leaders, are here to lead and supervise," Draga sneered, "and we don't have time to participate in committees. And we would like to have a word with you after the meeting. Now, if there aren't any other questions—"

"You don't have to worry about humans! You have my word!" said Goran loudly as he walked into the hall.

His appearance caused a great deal of confusion. All five dwarfs sitting at the leaders' table stood up abruptly. Most of the dwarfs were asking their neighbors if they knew who the human was and who had let him in. A few mothers pulled their children closer. Several dwarfs applauded, including the dwarf who had just been reprimanded.

"Seize him!" cried one of the leaders, "Guards! Guards!"

But before the guards could get to Goran, a sound appeared

out of nowhere. It grew louder and louder and as everyone was looking around to identify its source, the mine started to shake and parts of the ceiling started to collapse.

"Out!" cried Goran, "Get out of here! It's an earthquake!"

"Now, let's not overreact! We'll probably be safer here!" yelled Draga, but all her confidence had vanished. The earth continued to tremble although the sound had subsided. A few pieces of limestone detached from the ceiling and fell on the floor, barely missing the dwarfs standing underneath them. Goran, who decided he would not get a better opportunity, turned to the nearby families and cried as loud as he could, "Get your children out of here, or they will be buried alive!"

That seemed to have worked. Everyone rushed to the exit, as they continued to feel smaller but still persistent tremors. Goran quickly realized some of the dwarfs started to panic, tripping and falling as they ran for the exit. "Help me bring everyone safely outside," said Goran to the guards who had finally got to him, "and then you can seize me. I won't resist!"

The guards looked at each other, then looked around for their leaders, but all the leaders had already left the breakfast hall.

"We'll help you!" said the guard who had let Goran in the previous night, "if you don't tell our leaders we saw you last night."

"Deal!" said Goran.

A few minutes later everyone got outside safely. Goran and the guards were the last to exit the mine. When Goran finally got outside, he noticed it was unusually quiet. The dwarfs had circled around something and everyone was trying to take a look. When he finally made his way through the crowd, he stopped stunned. The sparse forest in front of him looked like covered with snow, but as Goran got closer, he realized he was looking at thousands and thousands of snowdrops covering the ground around the trees.

Goran had spent most of his life outdoors and had seen patches of snowdrops growing sporadically here and there, but nothing like this. For someone who had never seen the small white drooping bell of a snowdrop, the first herald of spring, the sight was overwhelming. Draga and the other leaders had stopped giving commands; the guards had forgotten about Goran. Even Goran was lost for words.

Suddenly, one of the dwarfs started clapping, which broke the light trance everyone seemed to have fallen into.

"Stamat!" exclaimed Goran, "What are you doing here? I thought you weren't coming!"

"I thought so too," replied Stamat, "but as I was flying away in the mortar—that's right, I have a mortar that flies"—Stamat paused to answer the question imprinted on a few astonished faces around him—" I noticed what seemed to me like a big area covered with snow. But since almost all snow in the area had melted, I was curious why there was still so much snow in this sparse forest. So I landed here to find this wonderful snowdrop field. I decided to wait and see if Goran would be able to bring any of you outside. After all, I could stay here for days—I don't mind the view! But then, there was that earthquake, and here you are."

Before Goran could respond, there was another light aftershock and the entrance of the salt mine finally gave in.

"Well," said Stamat, "I guess you are not going back in, not anytime soon!"

"It's all your fault!" screamed Draga. "Guards, seize them!"

"How is it our fault?" yelled Goran.

"Run!" screamed Stamat. "Do you still think you could reason with her!"

By the time the reluctant guards started chasing them, Goran and Stamat were already in the mortar shouting liftoff commands. Hundreds of longing eyes followed the initial wobbly takeoff and the subsequent smooth ascent.

"You can have this too!" shouted Stamat at the crowd as loud as he could, tapping on the side of the mortar, "but not if you continue to live underground."

"It looks like we failed again," sighed Goran.

"This is where you are very wrong, my friend." said Stamat. "Did you see the desire in the youngsters' eyes? Well, they will never forget the day they saw a flying mortar hovering over a snowdrop forest. And it's going to take much more than a few guards to stop them!"

"Do you think that God Veles had anything to do with the earthquake?" asked Goran.

"I guarantee you that he has everything to do with it!" smirked Stamat.

As usual, Stamat was right.

***

On his way to the Tree of Life a few hours earlier, God Veles thought that maybe it would be a good idea to stop and think of a plan before he entered God Perun's palace. At the same time, he knew this inner dialog would lead to no precautionary actions or investigation or any other sensible measures one would want to take if they were about to show up at the supreme god's abode and try to kill him.

God Veles was too ecstatic to think of details. He felt his newly-found freedom with every feather of his eagle self. His left talon clutched the golden apple tightly. No one and nothing could stop him now.

He reached the Tree of Life and flew in. God Perun was sitting by the big wooden table in the middle of the hall, almost in the same position the eagle left him at his last visit. He seemed lost in thought. The eagle glanced at the walls and was pleased to notice that the jars with the locked souls were still placed in the spots where he left them.

"Do you know where the golden apple is? I need to find a golden apple. Can you look for it?" said God Perun in a dry voice.

This sounded a bit strange to God Veles as he remembered God Perun asking the exact same question the last time he saw him. But he had neither the time nor the desire to ponder over this now. Without any hesitation, God Veles assumed his divine form.

"Perun!" he bellowed.

The god of thunder looked up, startled. His face froze in a

grimace of shock and dismay.

"Well," roared God Veles, "the good news is that, yes, I have found it! The bad news for you is that I have decided to keep it. And not only that, but I've also decided to put it to good use. It is I who deserve to be the supreme god of this land, and you, Perun, are more suitable for a different position—let's say the ruler of the Underworld? Well, now that I think about it, the Underworld already has a new ruler, but I am sure the two of you will work it out!"

Laughing, he casted the golden apple at God Perun.

The Tree of Life shook violently and a wave of destruction quickly radiated hundreds of miles away causing the surface of the earth to tremor. But the destruction on the tree that resulted from the impact surprised even God Veles. The spot where God Perun and the big wooden table used to be was now a gaping abyss. Startled, the souls flew frantically above him, their jars barely missing each other.

"Follow your new master!" bellowed God Veles, slightly disappointed he did not have to use them after all. "God Perun is your master now! God Perun is the new god of the Underworld and I am now the supreme god of this land! What are you waiting for? Follow him!"

God Veles stood on the edge of the abyss, hands pointing down as if to direct the swarm of souls to their last resting place.

CHAPTER 13
THE GOD OF THE UNDERWORLD

This time when something fell in the water, Vodnik did not bother to look at it. In the Underworld, lakes and rivers did not offer anything exciting. Whatever fell in the water was already dead. At first, Vodnik very much enjoyed being the new ruler of the Underworld and could not wait for the news to reach his cousin and main rival, the Great Vodnik of the Western Marshlands. But after a while, the thrill started to fade away. He missed the old days when he got great pleasure from drowning whatever alive would fall in the water—the bigger the better.

Morna, on the other hand, had no complaints. She had always had special bond with the souls in her father's jars. And now, she was surrounded by millions of souls. She quickly befriended quite a few of them, and they followed her everywhere. The newcomers found her presence especially comforting.

Vodnik was wrong to assume that whatever fell in the river was already dead. Somehow, the creature quickly resurfaced and started swimming toward the shore. The river was so wide and deep that it took it a few minutes to get out of the water. Vodnik was so shocked by what he was seeing that he just stood there quietly and stared at it. But nothing could prepare Vodnik for the shock he experienced when he realized that the creature was none other than God Perun.

The god saw him and waved him over urgently. Vodnik approached him cautiously. He had never interacted with the god of thunder and was not sure what to expect.

"Do you know where the golden apple is? I need to find a golden apple. Can you look for it?" said God Perun in a dry voice.

This struck Vodnik as a pretty unusual opening for a conversation. He was just thinking of a response, when he saw a dark cloud approaching from above. A moment later, he recognized his jarred souls and screamed with excitement, "My jars, my jars! I got them back!"

Then he turned to God Perun and said, "I don't have a golden apple, but you can have one of my jars! What are you doing here anyway?"

***

At the edge of the abyss inside the Tree of Life, God Veles was observing the last of the jars flying down the long tunnel that led to the Underworld. It was over! He, God Veles, was finally the supreme god of this land. Now all he needed to do was destroy the tunnel, although he was pretty certain the golden apple killed God Perun. His nemesis could not have survived an explosion of such proportions.

Then, he remembered that Vodnik and Morna were still there. Well, Vodnik had got what he wanted. After all, God Veles promised him the Underworld, not a trip back. And Morna... he really liked her. But he had the feeling she would rather live in the Underworld than in the World of the Living. And the dead did not use the Tree of Life to get to the Underworld anyway.

Maybe he could leave the abyss open and bring in Dragon Zmei to guard it. He remembered that Lamya killed him last summer, but he was sure he could find another one. They had always been very loyal to God Perun, but it was time for them to join their new master. Lamya, on the other hand, would be very distraught when she found out he had forgotten his promise to make her a goddess. How could she believe something so ridiculous! True—she saved his life on a few occasions, but he could not have truly died anyway. Maybe he could trick her and send her to the Underworld, so that she would not bother him anymore.

And he still had to find the last golden apple that was lost in the battle the previous summer. And he had to destroy all the golden apple trees to make sure nobody could ever get another golden apple again. Maybe he could look at the Book of History of Everything and try to find out what happened to that last golden apple. Although, he chuckled, God Perun, before his untimely death, was trying to do just that with no success. He looked around once again, but the Book of History of Everything was nowhere to be found.

Nevertheless, all this could wait. All he wanted to do now was get to the top of the Tree of Life—his new palace. He had never been to the top. God Perun was the only one who had access to it. But according to the rumors, it was unimaginably beautiful. There were stairs attached to the inner walls of the palace ascending at a forty-five degree angle. He supposed he could take his time and use them, tasting the victory with every step. But why wait? Patience had never been one of his virtues.

He flew up, ascending faster and faster toward the top. Halfway through his flight, the walls started to change. They looked more and more as if they were not made of any solid material, but rather looked like clouds with golden glow. He stopped for a moment to touch the wall, but it felt solid. Either this was a great optical illusion, or the matter the walls were made of hardened every time someone touched them.

He resumed his flight and, in a few minutes, reached the very top of the tree crown. The golden clouds under his feet were bathed in sunlight. It took him some time to get used to walking on the glowing substance without worrying that he would fall through.

Suddenly, he noticed something in the distance, and as he approached it further, he realized he was looking at the back of God Perun's throne. So this was where the former god of thunder kept his throne, not on the filthy earth underneath. The throne, which was made of solid gold, was decorated with rare and beautiful gems that even God Veles had no idea existed. The big round table in front of it was made of the purest white albite. Could the Book of History of Everything be lying on the table just an arm's length reach?

"You couldn't stay away from me, could you!" a strong voice bellowed as the throne revolved and positioned the owner of the voice right in front of God Veles.

God Veles was so shocked that he felt a strong wave of calmness spreading over him, most likely a self-defense mechanism to protect him from having a complete and permanent meltdown. At the same time, he became aware of the presence of a dozen or so Imperial Eagles perched on alabaster stands around the table.

"Hhhh...hhhhh," God Veles managed to mutter.

"I suppose you are asking how I got here after you killed me with a golden apple, and I fell in the tunnel that leads to the Underworld?" God Perun asked.

God Veles did not react.

"Well, it is a long story, but I am sure you won't mind hearing it. You see, after I found out you were plotting my demise, I realized I was not prepared to defend myself if you ever found one of the golden apples that got lost in our last battle. I had no golden apples left, as I melted them all and turned them into a golden string. And the golden apple tree was not to yield more apples until next fall. I became increasingly worried, especially after I read in the Book of History of Everything that Stamat had found one of the golden apples and had promised it to you. I started searching in the book frantically, day and night; I had to find where the last golden apple was, the one that was taken by the winds. But one day, after a very frustrating and futile night of reading, it hit me. I didn't really need a golden apple—I had my golden string. It had already helped me create thousands of saltwater species, and I very much enjoyed the process. I would have kept going if it wasn't for your obsession to destroy me and take my place. So I decided to create a double, a creature, who looks like me and acts like me well enough to fool you and make you waste your only golden apple on him. Not a decision I am proud of. It took me a few tries, but obviously I have succeeded."

God Veles did not respond. God Perun was not sure if his archenemy heard anything of what he said. God Veles was most likely not listening, but instead was thinking what to do next, because suddenly he turned into an enormous fire-breathing Dragon Zmei and attacked the unsuspected Imperial Eagles.

The birds took off in a panic, circling over the table with horrendous squawks. Some fell on the ground, scorched, dead or dying. By the time God Perun realized what was happening, God Veles had quickly turned himself into an eagle and mingled with the rest of the horrified birds.

God Perun was not willing to guess which one of the eagles was God Veles.

"Attack him!" bellowed God Perun, but the eagles were too afraid to turn against the eagle who had just killed a few of their own.

God Veles took advantage of this, dashed toward the Book of History of Everything, grabbed it with his talons, and flew away. God Perun flew after him, casting as much lightning as he could. Deafening thunder followed. God Veles had almost reached the entrance to the trunk of the tree and was about to start descending when a bolt of lightning struck him, burning most of his body and tearing the book into pieces. He was able to resume his divine form, but was too hurt to fly.

As God Veles fell toward the roots of the Tree of Life and

the Underworld, God Perun roared, "I am sending you to the Underworld where you belong, Veles, and you are to rule this and no other kingdom, forever and ever, until the end of time. And you will stay there until the day the sun swells and engulfs the earth in its fiery embrace!"

As God Veles was falling further and further down the Tree of Life, he was glad he could no longer hear God Perun. The narrowing roots somewhat broke his fall and he landed in the Underworld, badly burned and bruised.

He happened to crash right next to where Vodnik and his new acquaintance were standing. A few torn pages of the Book of History of Everything landed next to him seconds later.

"My Lord," exclaimed Vodnik, "what happened to you?"

God Veles saw God Perun's look-alike, jumped to his feet, and got behind him. His forearm squeezed on the creature's throat and did not let go until he felt the lifeless body slump down against his feet.

"My Lord! What did you do! This was God Perun!"

"No, it wasn't! It was his double! He tricked me!" cried God Veles, shaking with hatred and anger.

"You mean I could have drowned him?"

"Yes, you could have! You miss this whole drowning thing, don't you? Well, I have good news for you, Vodnik! Your services are no longer needed here! Get out of my kingdom!"

"My Lord!" gasped Vodnik.

It took a few minutes for this turn of events to sink into

Vodnik's mind.

"As you wish, my Lord," said Vodnik, trying to sound more disappointed than he really was. "I'll go find Morna."

"Your daughter can stay if she wants to. I will need someone to take care of the souls, especially the newly arrived. I was never good at consoling the dead. Somehow I could never relate to their problems!"

Vodnik knew how to find his daughter. All he needed to do was look for souls hovering together. Chances were they were hovering over Morna, listening to her stories or accompanying her on her long walks.

This time Morna was sitting on a big boulder by the Lake of No Return.

"And then my uncle, the Great Vodnik of the Southern Marshlands," he heard her saying to a few dozen souls, "invited my father to visit the Southern Marshlands, all the way down by the Sea of Marmara. My father had never seen the sea before. He was so excited to jump in its warm waters that he completely ignored my uncle's warning. Sure enough, not a moment later, my uncle heard my father screaming. My father's skin had turned to wrinkly leather. He could not breathe under the salty water, and on top of it, a big and particularly vicious stingray was chasing him."

A collective gasp filled the air. Vodnik smiled at the memory of his adolescent years. Parts of his skin were still damaged by the contact with the salt water that day, but it was worth the experience.

Vodnik realized he had been standing there for a while,

thinking about the past, while Morna had paused her story and everyone was waiting for him to speak.

"Morna," Vodnik finally said, "I need to talk to you. Alone."

"Give us a minute," said Morna to the souls.

The souls flew a few feet away, but felt something was amiss.

"Morna," said Vodnik, "God Veles has returned. Permanently. I suspect he had a fight with God Perun and lost. God Perun must have banished him to the Underworld because God Veles is here to stay and he doesn't need us anymore."

"What will happen to my friends? They need me!" whispered Morna. She did not want the souls to hear what she was saying, but they noticed her eyes filling up with tears.

"Well," hesitated Vodnik, "I didn't want to tell you this, because I knew what your decision would be, but you'll probably find out sooner or later. God Veles said you could stay if you wanted to. But I have to go."

Vodnik did not have the courage to look at her. For the first time in his life he felt a lump in his throat. This sensation was quite unpleasant and overwhelming, and he had to sit down.

"Father," said Morna, wrapping her hands around his head as she kneeled next to him, "You know how much I love you. I would give anything for us to stay together. But the Underworld is my home now. I feel like I belong here. I've never felt this way in the World of the Living."

"I know, my child," said Vodnik, stroking her pale face, "just like I couldn't live in a world I can't drown anyone..."

He felt a salty tear drop on his hand and burn his skin, but he did not react. Somehow the physical pain was helping him deal with that new unpleasant feeling still lingering in his chest.

Later, as he clumsily made his way to the World of the Living, he stopped and turned. Morna was sitting on the ground surrounded by a few dozen very well-meaning and compassionate souls who were going out of their way to cheer her up.

God Perun had had better days. Although he had defeated God Veles once and for all and banished him to the Underworld for all eternity, he had to spend most of the afternoon tending to the injured and dying Imperial Eagles. One eagle, who was lucky to escape unharmed, was sitting on an alabaster stand, looking at the pile of dead eagles and throwing reproachful looks at him.

"You know I can't do anything for the dead ones, Goritza," said God Perun. "I've told you before—even I can't reverse death!"

***

The horrific thunderstorm that day made Goran and Stamat abandon their flight back to Goran's village. Stamat landed the mortar not long after the ferocious storm started ripping through the otherwise clear skies.

"I have to go back to the Old Salt Mine," said Stamat. "This storm is about to undo everything we've done so far. Even the dwarfs we had no trouble convincing to leave the underground will think twice now."

"Do you think this storm has something to do with God

Veles and God Perun fighting again?" asked Goran.

"If I have to guess, God Perun is now retaliating at whatever God Veles did to him with that earthquake."

"Let's go," said Goran. "I am coming with you. Let's build a couple of huts close to the mine, but not right next to it, so that Draga won't be able to kick us out of the area. You are right. We don't have to wait until summer to come back. Strike while the iron is hot. That's what your people used to say, didn't they?"

"They sure did, Goran! They sure did!"

***

By the end of fall, most of the residents of the Old Salt Mine had left their underground homes with the help of Goran and Stamat, who shared with them everything they knew about life in the open. Word got around, and soon more and more dwarfs from other underground settlements joined in.

As the last of the trees were losing their brightly colored leaves, Goran was getting ready to return to his village. "Maybe I will stop by the Strawberry Cave and see if they need my help," he told Stamat.

"I could have never done it without you, Goran," said Stamat. "Everyone here will miss you, but I understand your decision. I will keep an eye on your hut and hope you'll visit us next summer."

"Hey, don't mention it. You and your father saved my life. I can never repay that!"

"Yeah, the good old days. You know, I wonder what ever

happened to God Veles. We haven't heard from him recently. Things have been pretty quiet. I am starting to get bored. I think I almost miss him," Stamat said, then laughed.

Stamat's laughter somehow caused a small nocturnal creature, fast asleep under a wet log in the outskirts of the Underworld, to wake up from his unsettling dream and shudder.

ABOUT THE AUTHOR

Milkana N. Mingels grew up in Bulgaria—an ancient land reigned by feuding Slavic gods and home of some pretty quirky characters, such as the not-to-be-trusted Baba Yaga, and the ridiculously good-looking samodivas. She heard stuff. And now she is telling it all.

www.ingramcontent.com/pod-product-compliance
Lightning Source LLC
Chambersburg PA
CBHW020247150626
46552CB00020B/641